REBEL PROTECTOR

A THRILLING, SECOND CHANCES, ENEMIES-TO-LOVERS ROMANCE

BLACKTHORN SECURITY
BOOK FIVE

GEMMA FORD

Rebel Protector

Copyright © 2024 by Gemma Ford

All rights reserved.

No part of this book may be reproduced in any form or by any electronic or mechanical means, including information storage and retrieval systems, without written permission from the author, except for the use of brief quotations in a book review.

Mortlake Press

ISBN: 978-1-7385403-6-5

First Edition

Cover design by Deranged Doctor

Disclaimer: This is a work of fiction. Names, characters, places, and incidents are the products of the author's imagination or used in a fictitious manner. Any resemblance to actual persons, living or dead, or actual events is purely coincidental.

CHAPTER 1

The wheels of the SUV left the tarmac and hit gravel. Ghost could hear it kicking up off the surface of the road, bouncing along and hitting the undercarriage. They must be nearly there. It had been a stifling hour-long drive from Panama City with his hands bound behind his back and a sack over his head, but he understood the need for secrecy.

Aleksandar Markov, the new kid on the block and one of the most ruthless arms dealers the region had ever seen, valued his privacy. His hacienda was situated on the Panamanian coast, in the middle of nowhere.

It had taken weeks of negotiation to reach this point. First, Ghost had used his contacts in the drug trafficking industry to get in touch with Markov's right-hand man, Luis Ramirez. Then, after being vetted and having his position in the trafficking network verified, he was granted a meeting with Markov.

They had picked him up outside his hotel in Panama City, a squalid hostel that barely deserved its single star, and brought him here—but not before he was patted down and checked for wires and weapons. Now, feeling disoriented and a little carsick, he had arrived at his destination: Alex Markov's secret hacienda. In a few moments, he'd meet the infamous legend himself.

Markov had arrived six months ago with a cache of illegal arms that he needed to offload. Where the weapons had come from, no one knew. Rumor had it they were from conflict zones in Eastern Europe and Central Asia, where he had a string of black-market contacts. But since the FBI was closing in on his operation, he'd packed up and relocated to Panama, where there was a lucrative trade in illegal arms to guerrilla groups, cartels, and paramilitary organizations in South America.

He had pissed off many established arms dealers in the region, but they had been swiftly dealt with in such a manner that no one was likely to challenge his position again. Markov was here to stay.

The SUV came to a halt, and Ghost heard the front passenger door open and someone get out. There were footsteps on gravel, and he braced himself for the unexpected. Always be prepared.

But nothing happened.

A moment later, his door opened, and he was hauled out of the vehicle. Once on his feet, the ties binding his wrists were cut, and the bag was ripped from his head.

Damn, it was bright.

He blinked to adjust his vision. As soon as he could see properly, he looked around, taking stock of his surroundings. They were outside a Spanish-style mansion in a stone courtyard with a fountain in the middle. The property was heavily secured. He immediately spotted two armed guards watching from a respectful but highly accurate distance, not counting the four banditos who'd brought him here, all of whom were packing.

The man who had put the bag over his head was called Carlos. He was an ugly motherfucker with a scowling face, a hawkish nose, and lips that seemed molded into a permanent sneer. Ghost didn't like him and sure as hell didn't trust him. He didn't know the names of the two thugs he'd cozied up with in the back seat, but they walked off, and the SUV drove around the back, presumably to park.

Ghost studied the lavish white Mediterranean residence with its typical, red-tiled roof. It was an impressive building, and what it lacked in height, it made up for in breadth. He suspected it stretched back a fair distance, probably all the way to the beach. He could smell the sea; it was no more than five hundred meters away. The salty tang was a welcome relief after the hot stench of Panama City.

The front door opened, and through the expansive archway walked a compact, stocky man in an expensive suit. His hands were clenched into fists, but he made this look natural. He practically sizzled with thinly concealed aggression.

"Mr. Ramirez?" Ghost inquired.

The man stretched out his hand. "Mr. Domínguez, welcome to Villa del Mar. I'm sorry for the crude method of delivery, but you know how it is…" He petered off with a non-apologetic shrug.

They shook hands. "I understand." For this assignment, Ghost was using his real name, since they were bound to do background checks on him. His legend was an extension of his own history, it was safer that way.

"Follow me. Mr. Markov is expecting you."

Ramirez nodded at Carlos before turning on his heel and heading back into the house. Ghost walked with him under the white arch and through a double-volume, steel-reinforced front door. No one was getting in here without an invitation.

The interior was cool and surprisingly tasteful. Marble tiles, white walls, and top-notch air conditioning all contributed to the ambiance. Luscious indoor plants were strategically placed in darker corners, and the walls were adorned with several pieces of fine modern art.

They descended a short flight of stairs to a formal living area, and through the floor-to-ceiling windows, Ghost caught a breathtaking view of the terrace and swimming pool. It was surrounded by natural vegetation, giving it a tropical feel. In the distance, he could see a partial view of the pearly sands of the estate's private beach. It was quite a secret hideaway Markov had here.

Reclining on a sofa, a finger of whiskey in a glass on the coffee table in front of him, was Aleksandar Markov himself. He didn't look anything like Ghost had imagined. After all the briefings, he had expected a monster. Instead, Markov was of average height, distinguished, and corporate-looking with a smattering of salt-and-pepper hair. He reminded him of a retired city banker.

"Mr. Dominguez, how good of you to come." He even sounded like a banker. His accent was interesting—a mixture of an American twang over a distinctly Eastern European inflection.

Ghost stepped forward and shook his hand. It was cool and dry, but the handshake was firm and strong. "Thank you for seeing me." It was the eyes, Ghost decided, that betrayed his ruthless nature. Pale blue and colder than the polar ice caps, they were totally devoid of emotion.

"Please, sit down. Becca will bring us some tea." He snorted. "A little habit I picked up when I lived in London many years ago."

Ghost glanced up and saw a stunning brunette hovering in the doorway. Glossy brown hair, soft curves, and legs that disappeared under a tight skirt that went on forever. She flashed him an efficient smile and nodded to Markov before disappearing to get the beverages.

Damn. Markov sure knew how to pick them.

Was he sleeping with her?

A stunner like that, Ghost couldn't see how he wasn't. Markov struck him as the kind of man who took what he wanted from life and to hell with the consequences.

Ghost turned his attention back to the arms dealer. "It's a beautiful place you have here. I'll bet the sunsets are something else."

Markov smiled and acknowledged the truth of that statement with a small bow of his head. "It's not California, but it'll do."

Ghost didn't respond. He'd been told Markov had been based in San Francisco, near Silicon Valley, where he'd funded some sort of crypto startup. Apparently, it had been a way to launder his blood money and allowed him to operate undercover on the dark web. Ghost didn't know much about those things, but he got the picture. Markov was a HVT and top of the FBI's Most Wanted list.

"Where do you hail from?" asked Markov. Ramirez poured himself a drink from a liquor cabinet, then took a seat at a modern glass-and-chrome table a few feet away. Markov's partner was an observer in this meeting, not an active participant. It was clear who called the shots.

"Florida, originally," Ghost replied, sitting down opposite the arms dealer. "Although I move around a lot."

Markov nodded. It was expected in his line of work.

"Tell me about that." Markov's gaze fixed on Ghost's face.

"About what?" Ghost knew what he meant, but he played along.

"How did you end up here, in Central America?"

It might seem like a harmless question, but it was an integral part of the interview. Markov had checked him out, but this was the part where he had to live up to his reputation—where he had to sell himself to Markov as someone the arms dealer needed.

"After I left the Army, I was assigned to the U.S. Training Support Unit in Belize as an instructor in close combat and jungle warfare. That was my specialty back in the military."

"Special Ops, wasn't it?"

Ghost was impressed. Markov had done his homework. The arms dealer must have contacts in the DoD to get that kind of information. Usually, Special Forces operatives' names were redacted for their own safety, even after they'd left the service. But that's why he'd used his own name, it could only help his cause.

"Yes, sir. I served ten years in the U.S. Marine Corps and four in MARSOC." MARSOC, or Marine Forces Special Operations Command, was the Marine Corps' special operations unit. They specialized in direct action, special reconnaissance, and counter-terrorism. Its members trained and operated closely with the more famous Navy SEALs.

Markov narrowed his eyes. "So, after fourteen years risking your life for your country, you end up an instructor in a rainforest in the ass end of nowhere? Is that right?"

Ghost gritted his teeth. That about summed it up. "Yes, sir."

"What did you do to piss them off?"

Ghost remained silent, his entire body tense. This was one step farther than he wanted to go, but he saw the value in it. He'd be a fool not to work this angle. Showing how angry he was about what had happened would sell his cover even more. The best part was, he didn't even need to lie about it.

The stunner returned with the tea and put the tray down in front of them. "Shall I pour, Mr. Markov?"

"Please, Becca."

She bent over, and Ghost caught a whiff of her perfume. It was light and sensual, like meadow flowers on a summer day. He watched as she poured tea into two china cups, admiring the way she moved. It was like sexy poetry in motion.

Her hair fell forward, but she made no move to tuck it back behind her ears. Suddenly, he wanted to touch it, to slide his hand around the back of her neck and draw her towards him.

Fuck, his fantasy was running away with him.

Sure, it had been a while since he'd had a woman, but still… Now? In the middle of an undercover op? He must need his head examined.

She handed him the tea with the barest hint of a smile. Her eyes were a rich brown flecked with gold, and where Markov's were empty, hers were filled with hidden secrets.

Then she did the same for her boss, this time adding milk and one sugar cube before stirring it thoroughly. How had she known Ghost took his black?

"She makes an excellent cup for a Yank," Markov remarked once she had left the room. Ghost noticed she hadn't offered Ramirez any. "That's one of the reasons I stole her."

"Stole her?" Ghost thought he'd misheard.

Markov laughed. "Nothing sinister, I assure you. I poached her from the U.S. Embassy in Panama City. I was there for a meeting, and she served us tea. It was perfect—very rare in this part of the world—so I made her an offer she couldn't refuse. Now she works for me, and to be honest, I couldn't do without her. Becca literally runs my life. Anyway, I digress. You were saying?" He turned his dead eyes back to Ghost.

Ghost didn't want to know exactly what Becca did for Markov, so he forged ahead with his cover story.

"I was in charge of an op that went south," he explained. "We received some bad intel and stormed an enemy hacienda, only to find it was a hospital for sick, orphaned kids. It was a major fuck-up. There were no casualties, thank God, but we got caught in one hell of a firefight on the way out. It became an international incident, and my team was held responsible." He couldn't keep the bitterness from his voice.

Markov watched him closely. "You took the blame."

"Yeah, I was the unit commander. I had no choice. Someone's head was going to roll, and it happened to be mine. I was offered the post in Belize because they didn't know what to do with me. I was an embarrassment to the squad—or to the politically motivated powers that governed the unit."

"Is that why you went AWOL?"

Now for the fun bit.

Ghost scoffed. "The salary was fucking abysmal, and there was no action. Why would I want to stay in that shithole when I could earn ten times that on the private circuit?"

"As a paid mercenary," Markov added.

"Of sorts," Ghost leaned forward, preparing for the hard sell. "Sir, I single-handedly set up Alberto Suarez's distribution ring through the notoriously dangerous Darién Gap between Panama and Colombia. I scouted the route, set up the network, bribed the locals, and then tested and secured it until it was perfect."

"Suarez was caught," Markov pointed out. "He was arrested two weeks ago by the DEA."

"Not on my watch," Ghost replied. "And not because of anything I did. He sold his product to the wrong guy—that's what got him busted. He walked straight into a trap. My distribution network is still in place." And therein lay the unique selling point and the sole purpose of this meeting. He let his words sink in.

Markov studied him for a full minute before he replied. "Is that why you're here? You want to work for me?"

Ghost took a deep breath. "Since Suarez is out of play, I'm out of a job. I hear you're looking to expand your distribution into Colombia, and I have those routes already in place. If I can speak plainly, sir?" He glanced at Ramirez and then back at Markov.

Markov nodded. "Whatever you need to say, you can say in front of Ramirez."

Ghost continued. "It's perfect for small arms distribution. There are no end-user certificates to forge, the disseminated nature of the network makes it much harder to police, the border is in the middle of impenetrable jungle, impossible to patrol in any orderly fashion, and the best part is, I know how to get the merchandise through without detection."

There was a pause as the relevance of what he was offering sank in. Ramirez glanced at Ghost and then to Markov, his eyebrows raised. Still, Markov didn't react.

Ghost waited. He picked up his teacup and took a sip. He wasn't the biggest fan, but Markov was right. It was excellently brewed.

"Who'd you hear that from?" Markov asked softly.

Ghost met his gaze. "From suppliers we used to deal with on the Colombian end. They told me they're interested in acquiring your weapons to support their cause."

Many of the drug cartels and criminal groups operating in Colombia purchased arms from dealers like Markov. Sometimes they paid with cocaine, other times with cold, hard cash. Either way, it was a lucrative business to be in. Markov was intent on muscling in, and Ghost was giving him his chance.

The pale blue eyes flickered over his face, but Ghost remained passive. He forced his shoulders to relax. "It's all set up," he reiterated. "You don't have to do anything other than sit back and enjoy the profits. There's a market that wants what you're selling, and I have a way to get it to them with minimal risk."

"It's worth considering," cut in Ramirez, speaking for the first time.

"How do I know you aren't full of shit?" Markov asked.

"Because I worked for Suarez for ten months and helped make him a very rich man. Ask anyone involved in his organization—they'll vouch for me."

"There aren't many left who aren't in jail," Markov retorted.

"Like I said, that had nothing to do with me."

"Why weren't you arrested?" Ramirez directed the question to him.

Ghost glanced at him. "Because I'm too smart to go along to a sting." Markov snorted. "My business was the supply end," Ghost continued. "I wasn't involved in selling the merchandise. My job was to bring in the product from Colombia, that's it. When I got wind of what had happened, I disappeared. There's nothing linking me to Suarez's organization."

"Smart." Markov drummed his fingers on the side of his empty teacup, his brow furrowed. The seconds ticked by. Eventually, he said, "Okay, I'm interested. Let's set up a trial run and see how it goes."

Ghost nodded.

He was in.

Becca, Markov's assistant, returned. "Is there anything else I can get you, sir?" Even her voice was sweet, like honey.

"We're good." He waved her away, and she left the room, but not before shooting a curious, appreciative glance in Ghost direction.

CHAPTER 2

*D*amn.

Becca fanned herself as she left the office. Why was she always attracted to the wrong type of guys? Outlaws, bad boys, surfer bums, you name it. If there was a badass in the vicinity, she was totally hooked. Even at school, she'd been attracted to the boy who smoked behind the bike shed or backchatted the teachers. It was a miracle she'd kept out of trouble herself. Right now, her hormones were buzzing, and she'd only served the guy tea!

Down girl, she told herself firmly. *He is off limits.*

That man oozed danger—she could see it a mile away. It surrounded him, from his deep-set dark eyes that held a thousand secrets, to the sharp line of his jaw. But he wasn't just some bad boy with attitude. He dressed like a soldier—khaki combat pants and a fitted T-shirt stretched to breaking point across his hard, muscular body.

Everything about him screamed mercenary.

Then there were his hands. Strong and capable, the kind that had taken the delicate china teacup from her but were clearly more at home gripping an assault rifle or submachine gun.

She'd seen his type before. Hell, this place was surrounded by armed guards 24/7. They were all ex-military, hardened warmongers. She blew a strand of hair out of her face. Except none of them looked like Domínguez.

He carried himself like a predator on the hunt—coiled, dangerous, always ready. She got the impression that he knew just how much trouble he was capable of and didn't care. He was the kind of man who took risks most wouldn't dream of—and still came out alive.

This one was trouble. And God help her, she liked it.

"Panama is a dangerous place," Markov had explained when she'd first started her job. "Many people don't want to see me succeed. That's why we have so much security, and why you have to live on the hacienda."

Despite her better judgment, she'd agreed.

To be fair, he was paying her a small fortune to be at his beck and call. She managed his house, hired and fired his staff—if he didn't fire them first—and organized his life so it ran like clockwork. In addition to playing housekeeper, she was also his unofficial secretary and tea girl. She even bought gifts for his mistress, a Colombian supermodel who lived in one of his Panama City apartments.

Becca enjoyed her job, trying not to dwell on the fact that she was, essentially, a virtual prisoner. Whenever she needed to go into town, one of the bodyguards escorted her, and she was blindfolded for the journey there and back.

"It's for your own protection," Markov had told her. "So that if you're kidnapped, you won't be able to lead anyone back here." It wasn't a comforting thought, but somehow appealed to her crazy, inexplicable attraction to danger.

One day she'd push it too far, she knew that, but so far, so good. Nothing untoward had happened, apart from a skirmish at the gate last month when a local man caused a fuss. He'd been swiftly dealt with, and there hadn't been any issues since. So, she put the risks out of her mind and focused on growing her bank account. When it came time to leave, she'd have a decent nest egg to start over with.

She watched from her office window as Domínguez was chaperoned out into the yard. He was a hulk of a man with wide shoulders and a commanding presence. Even from this angle, he sizzled with unbridled power.

Her eyes widened as Ramirez shook his hand. Now, that didn't happen very often, certainly not with just another employee. Ramirez was Markov's money man, and he didn't waste time talking to the security detail. He liked to think he was above all that, when in fact, his hands were just as grubby as Markov's.

Oh, she knew her boss was a crook. She'd have to be an idiot not to notice the shady deals, the late-night visitors, and the sleezy, nefarious characters he associated with. The official line was that he imported farming equipment from the U.S. and sold it to companies in Central and South America —but that was only a cover.

What he really did was something she preferred not to think about. It didn't impact her job, and it was in her best interest not to know too much.

Markov had once asked her how much she knew about his organization. It had been a loaded question, so she'd smiled sweetly and told him it was none of her business. He seemed to accept that and hadn't brought it up again.

That brute henchman of Markov's, Carlos, put a bag over Domínguez's head and guided him into the back seat of the SUV. She shivered at the memory of the times he'd done the same to her. He always managed to get in a grope or two once she was blindfolded—his hand brushing her breast or lingering on her back. And the way he leered at her... She knew what he wanted to do to her— not that he'd ever get the chance.

Now she took her own eye mask with her, so he had no excuse to touch her. That pissed him off, but she didn't care. The guy was a creep.

She guessed they were taking the bad boy mercenary back to Panama City. For some inexplicable reason, she was sorry to see him go. It wasn't just because he was a chiseled beast of a man that made her pulse race, or that when he'd fixed his dangerous dark eyes on her, her stomach had clenched with want.

No, it was something else. Something she couldn't quite put her finger on.

Curious, she pulled up the file she'd put together on him for her boss the previous week. Markov asked her to do background checks on all the men he hired. She'd even done one on his mistress, Adriana Sanchez, who apart from dating a minor drug dealer in 2015, was disappointingly clean.

Becca gave a soft snort. Her own past was shadier than that.

Her eyes scanned the screen. Ben Alfredo Domínguez, who went by "Dom," was an American. He'd left school at sixteen and enlisted in the U.S. Marine Corps. His father was a dock worker from Jacksonville, but there was no mention of his mother. With some additional digging, Becca had discovered she'd died in a car accident on the Gulf Coast when Dom was ten.

She blew out a breath. Tough break. That was one thing they had in common. She too knew what it was like to lose a parent.

He'd excelled in the Marine Corps, serving his country for ten years and completing an impressive four tours in the Middle East, all while working his way up the ranks. That was intense by anyone's standards. She could only imagine the things he'd seen.

Shortly after his last tour, he applied for the notoriously grueling MARSOC selection course. MARSOC, or Marine Forces Special Operations Command, was the Marine Corps' special operations unit. They specialized in direct action, special reconnaissance, and counter-terrorism. Dom had passed the course on his first attempt and was immediately deployed overseas. The specifics of those missions weren't clear, but that wasn't surprising—special operations missions were often classified. Even Markov's contacts at the Department of Defense couldn't access that level of detail.

Then came the botched operation that got him thrown out of the regiment. Again, there were no details. Afterward, he'd been reassigned to Belize, to a training center for U.S. Marines.

She stopped reading and leaned back in her chair, thoughtful. Why did a model soldier with an impeccable record suddenly go AWOL and end up working as a hired gun for a criminal like Alek Markov?

Had he simply had enough of being a lowly-paid instructor, or were there darker forces at play? Had he liked killing too much to be stuck in a training facility? Or was it the action that he craved? She'd probably never know.

Her phone buzzed. She glanced at the screen.

Markov. It was a summons.

She got up and went to his study, where he and Ramirez had closeted themselves after the meeting with Domínguez. She knocked on the door.

"Enter."

"You called, sir?" She never faltered in her professionalism or politeness when dealing with her boss, especially in front of his business partner and associates. It was a self-preservation tactic. Her efficiency sent the message that she was here to do her job, nothing more.

Alek Markov was an intensely private man, but the little she knew about him terrified her. It wasn't that he was a bully or treated her badly. It was his quiet ruthlessness that scared her. She'd seen how he dealt with people who crossed him, how he manipulated everyone around him. He'd arrived in the region six months ago and systematically annihilated the competition. Now, no one had the guts to challenge him.

He didn't know she knew, but it was impossible not to overhear some of his conversations when she brought in tea or biscuits.

And the staff talked. Fernando in the kitchen had become a friend, as had Maria, the young woman who cleaned the house every day. Both were from the nearby village and shared the rumors with her. Her boss had a very bad reputation. Alek Markov was not a man to be crossed—he had no mercy.

"I'm leaving town for a few days," Markov told her. "I need a flight to Colombia this evening, returning in two days. Hotel accommodation as well. That place we stayed at last time was decent enough."

"Will it be just you, or Mr. Ramirez as well?" she asked.

"Both of us," he confirmed.

"Yes, sir." She left the study, closing the door quietly behind her.

Two days in Colombia. This must have something to do with Domínguez's visit.

An uneasy feeling swept over her. That man was bad news, she could sense it.

What had they been discussing? What scheme had he been pitching to her boss?

Whatever it was, it involved the Colombians, and that

was never a good sign. It usually meant one of two things: drugs or weapons.

Maybe both.

She suppressed a shiver and logged back onto her computer.

She booked the flights to Bogotá and reserved two suites at the Sheraton, where they'd stayed before. Whoever her boss was meeting, it wouldn't be there. They'd meet somewhere off the grid. The kinds of people Markov did business with didn't like to be seen in public.

The file on Domínguez was still open on her computer. A photograph of him in his Marine Corps dress blues stared back at her. His shadowy eyes masked any emotion. His face was stoic, his shoulders back, head up—a proud man, back when he was still a respected member of the U.S. military. Now he was a rebel, a gun for hire, a soldier gone AWOL.

Did he still respect himself? Or didn't he care what he'd become?

She closed the window. The mercenary wasn't her concern, and as before, she'd probably never know.

CHAPTER 3

At four-thirty, Ghost left his roach-infested dump of a motel in Panama City and slunk into the back alley, which stank of piss and rotting garbage. The sun was still beating down, baking everything in a relentless heat that made his shirt cling to his back and sweat run into his eyes.

He paused, scanning the street, waiting. Markov's crew might've put someone on him. His instincts, honed by years of service, were sharp. Nothing moved. No one followed. Satisfied, he stepped out of the alley and onto the cracked pavement behind the motel. This wasn't the safest part of town, so he kept an eye out for both petty criminals and Markov's hired guns. The Glock tucked into the back of his jeans felt like a steady companion, just out of sight but always within reach. The military knife strapped to his ankle gave him a little more reassurance. He could handle himself, no problem—but he didn't need that kind of distraction right now. Too much was riding on this job.

He headed toward the intersection, took a right, and walked three blocks to a run-down bar that catered to the desperate and dangerous. Before stepping inside, he circled the block, checking for tails. No one was on him.

The door creaked as he pushed it open, the stale, smoky air hitting him. No one gave a damn about non-smoking laws here. His eyes adjusted quickly to the dim light, and he spotted his contact—a man in his forties with close-cropped hair and a lean, hard build, sitting at the back. Even in his casual jeans and loose shirt, Pat had *ex-Navy SEAL* written all over him. You couldn't scrub that kind of training off.

Ghost ignored the suffocating heat that only worsened in the bar. A ceiling fan whined and groaned as it made slow, useless rotations, and there wasn't a whiff of air conditioning to be found. The old man hunched over the bar didn't seem to mind as he worked his way through a bottle of Jack. Ghost's eyes swept over the room, instinctively assessing threats. A couple making out in the corner, a group of barely-out-of-their-teens drinking cheap beer and chain-smoking, and three guys playing a drinking game, a bottle of tequila between them. None of them set off any alarm bells.

"Pat." Ghost nodded at the man he'd met once before and slid into the chair across from him.

Pat returned the nod, tapping his beer. "Drink?"

"Yeah." Ghost didn't really want one, but it'd look off if he didn't.

Pat gestured to the barman, a pock-faced Panamanian with long hair who looked like he'd stepped out of a bad Tarantino flick. No table service here. When the beer landed on the counter, Ghost got up, grabbed it, and returned to the table, giving the barman a quick nod.

"How'd it go?" Pat asked, cutting right to the chase. Small talk wasn't in the playbook for men like them.

Ghost had first met Pat about a month ago, and it hadn't been under the best circumstances. The former Navy SEAL had caught him off-guard—something that didn't happen often. Ghost had been exhausted after a week in the jungle, heading back to his shabby apartment for a much-needed shower and some sleep when Pat and another guy named Blade had ambushed him. They'd been quick, well-trained, and Ghost had barely gotten in a swing before he felt the cold steel of a gun pressed into his back.

"We need to talk, Major," Pat had hissed.

It had been a long time since anyone had called him that. They'd forced him up to his apartment, and as soon as he realized who they were, Ghost knew he'd have to move. If these guys could track him down, so could anyone else.

Pat and Blade weren't amateurs—they were with Blackthorn Security, a private security outfit run by former SEALs that operated in the shadows.

"I'm impressed," Ghost had commented back then, but the two hadn't even cracked a smile.

"There are people worried about you," Pat had growled, keeping his weapon trained on Ghost.

"There always are," Ghost had shrugged.

"You've been off the grid for ten months. Your superiors want answers."

"I'm undercover," Ghost had growled. "They know that."

Pat had exchanged a glance with Blade. "I don't think they do. Your last contact was six months ago."

"I've been busy."

"There are rumors you've turned," Pat had added, his steel-gray eyes boring into Ghost. "Working for Suarez."

Ghost had scoffed. "Of course I'm working for him. That's my assignment."

"You can see how it looks," Pat had said. "Undercover operative gets cozy with one of Latin America's biggest drug traffickers, goes rogue. Why didn't you check in?"

"Too risky. I've earned Suarez's trust. Blowing that would've cost me the mission—and my life."

The two men had been dangerous, no question, but Ghost could hold his own. He'd kept his voice low, calm, even as they stared him down.

"You can trust us," Blade had said.

"No offense," Ghost had replied, "but I don't know you from Adam."

"SEAL Team Six," Blade had said, his voice clipped. "And this is Pat Burke, retired Navy SEAL commander. We run Blackthorn Security. We specialize in off-the-book ops."

"Among other things," Pat had added, his jaw hard enough to crack granite.

Ghost had studied them, weighing his options. "What do you want with me?"

Pat had grinned, a smile that didn't reach his eyes. "Glad you asked. We want to use your in with Suarez to infiltrate an arms dealer's operation. A guy named Alek Markov."

"I've heard of him. New guy, ruthless."

"That's him," Pat had confirmed.

"What's he done to you? This isn't your turf."

Pat's face had darkened. "He's involved in illegal arms deals—and he went after one of our own. We plan to take him down."

Ghost had leaned back, considering. "He's a hard man to get close to. Lives in a secret hacienda, guarded around the clock. His mercs are paid well enough to keep their mouths shut."

"You got to Suarez," Blade had pointed out.

"Suarez recruited me," Ghost had reminded them.

Pat had nodded. "We know you were sent undercover to figure out who was recruiting soldiers from the academy. That mission's done. It's time to move on."

"And Suarez?" Ghost had asked. "I've worked too long to bring him down. I deserve to be there when it happens."

"With your intel, the FBI will arrest him. But you can't be involved in the takedown."

Ghost had slammed his fist on the table, frustration boiling over. "After all the shit I've put up with, you expect me to just walk away? That bastard deserves more than a pair of cuffs."

Pat had leaned in, his voice steady. "This isn't your fight anymore, soldier. You're needed for something bigger—Blackthorn's mission has been sanctioned by the government. We need you to shift your focus to Markov."

Ghost had clenched his jaw. "You'll take Suarez down?"

"The FBI will handle him—and his entire organization. We just need you to give us the details of his next shipment."

Blade had chimed in then. "Once that's done, you'll disappear for a bit before making your move on Markov. Use your rep as one of Suarez's top guys to slide into his circle."

"And why would Markov hire me?"

Pat had smirked. "I'm sure you can think of something."

Ghost quirked his lips. "I think I have an idea."

GHOST TOOK a swig of the beer the pockmarked barman had set in front of him and grimaced at the taste. "I've made contact with Markov."

Pat eyed him curiously. "You went to his hacienda?"

"Yeah, but not without getting searched and hooded. They weren't taking any chances."

Pat leaned back in his chair, clearly impressed. Markov was known for his paranoia, keeping anyone he didn't trust at arm's length. "How'd it go?"

"He's agreed to a trial run." Ghost kept his voice low. "I convinced him that the network I set up to smuggle Suarez's narcotics into Panama could be used in reverse to transport Markov's weapons into Colombia."

"And is that actually doable?" Pat asked, seriously.

Ghost shot him a look. "You think I'd set this up if it wasn't?"

Pat chuckled. "Fair point. When's this trial shipment going down?"

"That's still up in the air," Ghost replied. "Markov needs to get back to me with the details, but I suspect he'll want to secure an order with the Colombians first. Still, we don't have to wait for that. My network's still in place, but they've heard about Suarez getting nailed, so I'll have to head down there, smooth things over. Make sure we're still good to go."

Pat's brow furrowed. "You think they'll spook?"

Ghost shook his head. "Nah. Most of them are indigenous—farmers, fishermen, regular folk who need the cash. Suarez going down puts them out of work. They'll come to the table."

Pat ran a hand through his short-cropped hair, shaking his head. "Hell of a way to make a living."

Ghost shrugged. Around these parts, it was just business. These guys made more in a week trafficking drugs and weapons than they ever did working the land. And no one knew the jungle better than they did. It wasn't complicated—it was survival.

"When do you leave?" Pat asked.

"Tomorrow. I'll be off the grid for about a week. No cell service where I'm headed."

Pat nodded. "Check in when you're back. Anything else you need?"

Ghost hesitated for a beat. "Actually, there might be another potential source of intel."

Pat raised an eyebrow. "Oh?"

"A girl—well, a woman." Ghost corrected himself, the image of that tall, leggy brunette flashing in his mind. Her scent had clung to him, a heady mix of wildflowers and something more dangerous. "She works for Markov. I'm pretty sure she's his personal assistant. American. Name's Becca. Word is she used to work at the U.S. Embassy in Panama City."

Pat nodded slowly. "I'll see what I can dig up on her."

"She might be useful. Markov told me himself he couldn't run his life without her."

Pat shot him a warning look. "Careful. She could be his mistress. Markov's not the type to share."

Ghost's jaw clenched. "Yeah, I've thought about that. I'll check it out before making any moves."

Their conversation wound down after that, each man knowing there was a lot left to do before Ghost would see Markov—or Becca—again. But as they parted ways, a surge of anticipation twisted in his gut. He couldn't shake it.

He shouldn't be this excited to see *her* again.

That kind of thinking was dangerous. He wasn't a man who got distracted easily, especially not by a woman. But something about Becca had burrowed under his skin. Her caramel eyes haunted him, like she was hiding something—maybe something big.

Was she really just a personal assistant? Or did she know things that could help bring Markov down?

Was she loyal to him, or was there room to manipulate her into giving them what they needed?

Whatever the case, he knew one thing for sure—he was looking forward to finding out.

CHAPTER 4

*B*ecca heard the car pull up and drifted over to the window.

It was *him*. He was back.

A frisson of excitement shot through her, like a live wire under her skin.

He's a bad boy, Becca. A thug.

She stared, unable to look away. His thick, bulging arms had probably gunned down more men than she'd care to know, those broad, mountainous shoulders carrying more than just gear—maybe wounded comrades, maybe bodies. And that hard, powerful body of his? It looked like it was built for chaos. Destruction.

Stay clear!

Yet her feet stayed planted. She watched as Carlos yanked the hood off his head, revealing Dominguez's face—hard, unyielding, and tense. He blinked in the sunlight, his eyes adjusting before he grabbed a bulging backpack from the car like it weighed nothing and tossed it over his shoulder. The way he moved, the way he carried himself—it screamed *soldier*.

Again, Ramirez came out to meet him, guiding him into the house.

Preferential treatment. He must be important to Markov.

Becca peeled herself away from the window, busying herself with the vase of magnolias on her desk, though her mind was far from the task at hand. The spacious office leading to Markov's study was where she spent most mornings, but this afternoon, she was restless.

She'd been told to prep the guest cabin down by the beach. Was Dominguez staying this time? Anticipation fizzed in her belly.

What is it about this guy?

He was no different than the other hired muscle wandering around. Big, dangerous, and lethal. The kind of man who exuded that arrogant confidence only someone who knew how to kill—and had done it—could carry. And yet, she couldn't shake the electric buzz that seemed to settle under her skin whenever he was near.

Get a grip, she told herself, snorting softly. It wasn't like he was the first man around here with a gun. This was the Americas, after all.

No, it was something else. The way he carried himself—with a quiet pride, like he knew he was a professional. His eyes didn't just scan the room—they observed. They had locked onto her the moment they met. And despite his rough exterior, she sensed a sharpness, an intelligence lurking beneath.

Maybe that's why Markov was working with him. Her boss didn't waste time on idiots. He liked precision and power, and maybe this guy had both.

Or maybe I'm imagining all of it, she thought, irritated. He was probably just another thug in the end, another mercenary with more brawn than brain. Just because he was built like a god and had eyes that reminded her of the jungle after the rain didn't mean he wasn't as hollow as the rest of them.

"Hello again," came a low, gravelly voice from the doorway.

Becca startled, her heart leaping into her throat. She'd been expecting him, but his presence still hit her like a jolt from a live wire. She spun around, flashing her best professional smile. "Good morning, Mr. Dominguez. It's good to see you again."

Their eyes locked, and for a second, she felt like she couldn't breathe. His gaze was intense, too sharp, too penetrating.

"Mr. Markov will be with you shortly," she added, her voice coming out more breathless than she intended.

He grunted and sank onto the sofa opposite her desk, stretching his long legs out in front of him, his frame dominating the room. Even with the massive mahogany desk between them, she felt the weight of his presence like a gravitational pull. His backpack landed with a thud beside him, reminding her just how lethal this man was.

"I have something to attend to," Ramirez said, and Dominguez gave a brief nod as the financier left the room.

Carlos, the sleazy head of security, took up his post by the door, his beady eyes watching everything. No matter how important Dominguez might be, trust was a rare commodity here.

"Can I get you anything?" The man practically radiated danger, and yet she couldn't stop herself. "Tea, coffee, a cold drink?" Damn, her voice sounded much too eager.

"I'm good," he muttered, his gaze fixed on her like he was appraising something far more personal.

Becca's pulse quickened. She gave him a tight smile and shifted in her seat, her fingers fumbling over her phone as she texted her boss to let him know Dominguez had arrived. She had to retype it twice—her fingers were shaky, damn it.

She was no stranger to powerful men, but there was something about Dominguez that got under her skin, made her feel exposed. His gaze wasn't just focused—it was consuming, like he could see straight through her, peeling back layers she wasn't ready to share.

A few agonizing minutes passed before her boss's office door finally swung open.

Markov appeared, as polished as ever in his tailored suit. His eyes flicked to Dominguez, sizing him up. After a brief pause, he nodded toward the study.

Dominguez stood, casting one last, lingering glance at Becca, before following Markov inside.

Becca let out a long breath. The room felt oddly empty without him, but at least her heart rate had a chance to slow down. She absently brushed a hot strand of hair off her forehead and tried to focus on the legal documents she'd been working on—farming equipment, her boss's "legit" business. Yeah, right.

It was no use. Her thoughts were elsewhere, swirling around the dangerous mercenary currently holed up with her boss. What the hell was his deal? Was he really just another hired gun? And why did it matter so much to her?

She sighed, giving up on the document for now. Once Dominguez was gone, maybe she'd be able to concentrate.

Twenty minutes later, her phone buzzed with a request for tea. Tea for two. Of course. Markov had found a kindred spirit in Dominguez. Both ex-soldiers, cut from the same lethal cloth.

She gathered the tray and entered the study, her movements practiced and smooth. The men paused their conversation as she walked in, but not before she caught the words "merchandise" and "distribution."

Her lips tightened into a forced smile. She didn't need to guess what kind of business they were talking about.

She set the tea down with precision, but before she could pour, Markov waved her off. "I'll handle it, Becs."

Becca nodded, avoiding Dominguez's intense gaze as she hurried from the room.

An hour later, the door swung open, and the two men emerged.

Carlos straightened, eyes sharp, and Becca watched as a silent nod passed between Markov and his guard.

Dominguez had passed whatever test this was.

He was now part of the crew.

"Becca, show Mr. Dominguez to his room," Markov instructed, his voice casual. "He'll be staying with us for a while."

Her stomach knotted as she stood, but she smiled, slipping into her professional role. "Of course. This way, Mr. Dominguez."

"There are some house rules," Markov added in a no-nonsense tone. Dominguez turned slowly, his movements deliberate, like a predator sizing up its prey.

"No weapons on the premises. That includes knives. Carlos will take care of anything you've got."

"Understood," Dominguez replied, his voice cool.

"Also, you are welcome to any member of my staff, should you get the urge, but my assistant, Becca, is off-limits."

Becca flushed. She knew it was for her own safety, but it gave their guest the wrong impression. Dominguez scowled, but didn't glance at her. He gave a tight nod.

Becca's face burned as she led the way out to the terrace, trying to keep her breathing steady. The sun was beating down, glistening off the swimming pool.

"How long will you be staying, Mr. Dominguez?" she

asked, keeping her tone polite as they walked around the pool.

"Hard to say," he replied vaguely. "I'll be coming and going."

That was new. Guests weren't usually granted that kind of freedom. Even she needed clearance from Carlos to leave the hacienda.

"Well, I hope you enjoy your stay," she said, her voice strained.

They walked down a narrow trail toward the beach, the vegetation brushing against their arms and legs. "Can you believe this was cut back just last week?" She swiped a branch out of her way. "It grows like wildfire."

He didn't respond. Of course he didn't. Guys like him didn't do small talk.

She led him toward a clearing where the guest cabins stood on stilts, all in a neat row. "The beach is through there," she said, gesturing toward a wide, sandy path. "And the only way back to the main house is the way we came."

"Unless you cut through the bush," he countered. She sensed a hostility in him that wasn't there before.

She gave him a glance. "Well, sure, if you like creepy crawlies."

"Nothing I haven't seen before," he muttered, his eyes scanning the dense foliage.

Tough guy, huh.

Of course. She bet he'd be comfortable living in the jungle for weeks on end. "You can try that, if you wish, however, there are security patrols operating on the premises. I wouldn't surprise them, if I were you."

"I've seen them."

She smiled. "Hard not to."

"Doesn't it bother you?" he asked suddenly, his gaze piercing.

"Doesn't what bother me?"

"Being trapped here, on the estate?"

"Not at all," she lied. "It's part of my job." She lifted her chin. "Besides, I'm not locked in. I can leave whenever I want. It's just for safety."

"Is that what he told you?" His voice had a sharp edge to it, like he didn't quite believe her.

Her smile slipped. "Let me show you around."

He followed her up the few steps, a hulking presence behind her, keeping her on edge. Once inside, she pulled the string attached to the ceiling fan, and the slow blades began stirring the heavy, humid air.

"If you leave the patio doors open, there's a nice breeze," she said, making idle conversation until she could regain her composure. "The kitchen is pretty basic, but if you need anything, just let me know."

He dropped his backpack on the floor with a loud thud. Startled, she flinched. He'd done that on purpose to unnerve her, she knew it.

"How do I reach you?"

She took a steadying breath. "You can call or text me. Here's my card."

"Becca Lyndall," he read, rumbling over the syllables. A shiver tingled down her spine.

"That's me," she said, the words catching in her throat. "Okay, well, if there isn't anything else—"

He didn't move, just stared at her, his intense presence seriously messing with her karma.

"If there is, I'll let you know." His unreadable gaze trailed after her as she stepped outside.

CHAPTER 5

"My man in Colombia has received the trial shipment," Markov announced, breaking into a grin.

Ghost sat across from him, already knowing this from the message his own contact had sent him that morning. Miguel, a local farmer and key player in the operation, had kept him in the loop. Ghost had to stay ahead of the game—always.

It'd been five days since he'd moved into the Villa del Mar hacienda, but only two of those days were spent lounging by the beach. The other three? Deep in the Panamanian jungle, making sure the trial run went off without a hitch. He couldn't afford to screw this up.

Miguel had collected the merchandise—just one crate for the trial—from a tribal fisherman who'd navigated the swampy waterways like it was second nature. The handoff had been smooth, ending with the crate stashed in an old warehouse on Miguel's sugar plantation outside Cartagena.

Everyone got paid well for their part, and that's how Ghost kept them loyal. No need for threats or bribes—just cash, and on time. So far, everything was running like clockwork.

Ghost reached across the desk and shook Markov's hand. "Good to hear. Let me know when you're ready to talk about scaling up."

Markov stroked his chin, looking every bit like a cliché Bond villain. "I've already spoken to the Colombians. We should get the green light any day now."

Ghost gave him a nod, keeping his expression calm.

Stay cool.

But inside, his mind was working overtime.

Get proof, Pat had drilled into him. *We need something solid.*

That was the tricky part.

The paperwork would be under dummy corporation names, signed by fake directors who probably didn't even know what they were putting their names on. It was airtight. No accountability.

That's how Suarez had run things. Nothing ever traced back to him. In the end, the only thing that brought Suarez down was the sting. He'd shown up in person for the final deal, and the whole thing had been caught on tape. No wiggle room after that.

Maybe that's how they'd get Markov, too. But Ghost wasn't counting on it. He needed another angle.

His mind wandered to Becca, sitting in the office next door.

Maybe *she* was the angle.

They hadn't exactly gotten off on the right foot. He still wasn't sure if she was sleeping with Markov. The way the arms dealer called her "Becs" rubbed him the wrong way—way too familiar. And the fact that Markov had made it clear she was off-limits? That screamed *possessive*.

Still, she didn't strike Ghost as the type. He was good at

reading people, and if he had to bet, he'd say she wasn't sleeping with the boss.

What the hell? It was worth a shot.

Worst case scenario, she shut him down. Wouldn't be the first time. He'd survive.

But best case? Maybe she wasn't off-limits after all. Maybe Markov was just pissed because he couldn't have her himself.

Ghost needed to up his game. He hadn't been in the seduction business in a while—ever since he'd left the force, it wasn't exactly high on his priority list. His pride had taken a hit after getting booted from his unit and stuck training fresh recruits in Belize.

But here? Now? The challenge had a spark to it. He was more than a little rusty, sure, but excited. And it wasn't just about getting laid. It was the success of the mission. Becca could be a key to getting inside Markov's operation.

Problem was, he had to make his move without security or cameras catching on. And let's face it, subtlety wasn't his strong suit.

Back when he was a Marine, it had been easy—he and his buddies walked into a bar, and the women hit on *them*. But this was different.

This was an undercover op.

And Becca wasn't some groupie hanging out at the bar. She was beautiful, sassy, intelligent. That made it tricky.

She thought he was a mercenary, a thug. He could see it in the way she carried herself around him—polite, but tense. Careful. Always careful. A hands-off vibe.

She's not wrong, he thought, grimly. He could be violent. But not in the way she assumed. His violence had purpose—quick, precise, and when necessary. No extra frills.

Still, there was a spark. He saw it in her eyes, no matter how much she tried to hide it behind those polite smiles. The way she looked at him sometimes, those caramel eyes with flecks of gold, her breasts thrust out defiantly, nipples taut against the fabric of her silk blouse.

Fuck. She made him hotter than he'd been in a long time.

The question was, how to turn that spark into an ember, and then that ember into a flame?

First things first—he needed to get her alone.

"Where's the cache now?" Ghost asked Markov later that afternoon. He'd heard rumors the arms dealer had a stockpile stashed away in a secret facility. He needed to know if it was close, just in case he had to act fast. "Is it nearby?"

But Markov wouldn't give up much, not yet. The guy was paranoid, and with good reason.

"It's close enough," came the short reply. "I'll give you access once we get the go-ahead."

Ghost nodded. That was enough for now. He had no idea how Markov had gotten his hands on these weapons, but he was sure none of them would trace back to the man himself. That was how these guys operated—clean hands, dirty deals.

"I'm heading into town to send a message to my guys this side of the border," Ghost said, watching Markov's reaction. He didn't want to be babysat by that slimy security lapdog, Carlos. Surely, Markov trusted him enough by now? "I'll take the usual precautions."

Markov leaned back, watching him carefully. "Carlos will drive you."

Ghost clenched his jaw. *Fuck.* He'd have to eat this one. Patience was key—just like with Suarez. It'd take time to earn full trust, and he needed to play the long game here.

"Sure," he said, biting back his frustration. "If that's the way you want it."

He left Markov's office, pulling the door shut behind him.

As he walked into the main hallway, his eyes fell on Becca at her desk, her fingers tapping away on the keyboard. Did she know that her boss was an arms dealer? Hell, maybe she handled all the paperwork—kept track of orders, shipments, the kind of stuff that wouldn't see the light of day.

He didn't know how deep she was in. But she didn't seem like the type to get her hands dirty. *Still... you never know.*

The place was quiet, no one else around. He took his shot. "I'm heading into town, if you want a ride."

She glanced up, her big brown eyes locking onto his. "Alone?"

He grimaced. "No. Carlos is tagging along."

She paused, biting that full lower lip, the pink flesh caught between her teeth. God, it made him want to be the one nibbling at her mouth, tasting her. His breath hitched, heat curling low in his gut.

Get a grip. If just looking at her was this distracting, how the hell was he going to pull off seducing her?

"Let me check with Alek—uh, Mr. Markov."

His jaw tightened at the way she called him *Alek*. That felt too familiar, too casual. Was he reading this wrong? *Were* they together?

His scowl deepened as he watched her stand up, smoothing down her skirt as she moved. She knocked on Markov's door and slipped inside.

Ghost couldn't help but strain to hear the conversation. Their voices were muffled, but something about it rubbed him the wrong way. When she came back out, her expression gave nothing away.

"I'm good to go," she said, brushing a strand of hair behind her ear. "When are you leaving?"

"Twenty minutes," he replied, his tone gruffer than he meant it.

"I'll meet you outside."

. . .

They set off, both blindfolded. Becca with one of those cushy eye masks you get on a plane, and Ghost with the same old crude hessian sack. He was getting used to it by now.

The first few times, it had been suffocating—brought him back to when things went sideways in Basra. He and his teammate had just dropped two CIA agents at the Kuwaiti border when their vehicle got flagged at a police roadblock. They were marched to a ratty outhouse beside the checkpoint, stripped, handcuffed, and blindfolded. The bag over his head had smelled just like this one—sour with the stink of sweat and fear.

But that wasn't even the worst of it. As the SUV rumbled over the dirt track, Ghost's mind flashed back to the van they were shoved into and the cold, grimy cell they were tossed in at the police station. That's when the mock executions started.

Each time the muzzle pressed against the back of his skull, he'd braced for his brains to be blown across the room.

Then—*click*. Nothing. Except their laughter, taunting him, soaking in his terror.

Closest I've ever come to death, he thought, grinding his teeth.

To shake it off, he breathed in Becca's soft floral scent, just inches from him. She was strapped into the seat next to him, and even though they weren't touching, her presence hit him like a jolt.

He hadn't seen the driver, but he'd glimpsed Carlos in the front passenger seat, gun resting on his lap, right before they'd bagged him.

Ghost found it odd they were cruising in such a top-of-the-line SUV. The thing was a bullet magnet. If it were him, he'd pick something local, something low-key. But, hey, this wasn't his op.

When they hit the city, they were finally told they could ditch the blindfolds. Ghost ripped off the bag, exhaling hard, pushing those bad memories down deep. He glanced at Becca as she quietly removed her mask, slipping it into her purse with practiced ease.

The rest of the ride was silent, but Ghost was hyper-aware of her beside him. He looked at her hands, fingers delicate and manicured. She took care of herself, and he liked that. Her cream skirt hugged her legs, and he could just make out the shape of her thighs beneath the fabric. She wore a soft pastel blouse tucked neatly in, and her sandals showed off those toned calves.

Everything about her screamed grace, beauty. Not exactly the kind of woman who'd be caught dead hanging out with a thug like him.

"Carlos, can you drop me at the market?" Becca asked, as they passed a bustling street lined with stalls. Ghost figured, having worked at the U.S. Embassy, she knew the place better than he did.

"That works for me," Ghost added, trying to sound casual.

Carlos glanced back at him through the rearview mirror and gave a nod.

Now came the tricky part. He had to find a way to spend some time with her without looking like a total idiot. He couldn't just come out with something cheesy like *"Hey babe, wanna grab a coffee?"* That would get him laughed out of town.

Besides, he wasn't the type of guy women like her went for. She was elegant and put-together, and he was, well... rough around the edges. A brute. Someone she probably wanted to steer clear of, not get close to.

Problem was, he wanted her close.

The SUV pulled to a stop near the crowded market, and they both climbed out. The street was lined with rows of makeshift stalls selling everything from fresh produce to colorful trinkets and hats.

"Can you pick me up outside the *supermercado* later?" Becca asked Carlos. "I'll have bags of stuff with me."

Carlos gave her a short nod, then gestured for the driver to pull away.

Perfect. That was his opening.

"See ya," Becca said, throwing him a polite, almost awkward smile as she turned to walk away.

"Wait," Ghost called after her, his heart beating faster than it should.

She stopped, frowning as she looked back at him.

"I've got some things to take care of, but when I get back, I can help you with the shopping."

Her eyes widened, like she hadn't expected the offer. "Really? Oh, um, okay. Thanks."

Had no one ever offered to help her before? Shopping for Markov's household must be a full-time job on its own, not to mention all the supplies for the staff.

"How about I meet you outside the supermarket in an hour?" Ghost suggested, trying to keep his voice steady.

She hesitated, then gave him a small, tentative smile that lit up her eyes. "That sounds good."

His heart did a little flip, and he found himself grinning like a fool. "Great. See you then."

Before he could embarrass himself further, he turned on his heel and strode away, feeling like a damn schoolboy who just got a date to the prom.

GHOST WALKED the few blocks to the seedier side of the city, where he was set to meet his contact. Jesús ran a small import-export business, but it was his brother, Pedro, who was the real prize. Pedro worked for the National Border Service, and between the two of them, they smuggled contraband over the border like pros.

They'd been a vital part of Suarez's drug network, and now that the cash flow had dried up, the brothers were hungry to get in on Markov's operation. With Ghost running point, they knew they'd be paid on time and paid well.

"Weapons are lower risk than drugs," Jesús had said before the trial run. "Sniffer dogs can't pick them up."

Ghost met him in a dingy café by the canal, the kind of place filled with grimy dockworkers, all sweat and cigarette smoke. Ghost, with his unshaven face and worn-out T-shirt, blended right in.

They hashed out the details—shipment logistics, handover points, and the routes through the jungle. It was a more substantial load this time, and they'd be using multiple middlemen, which would make it tougher for the authorities to trace.

A logger would haul the cargo on his truck deep into the rainforest. From there, a tribal fisherman would pick it up, navigate the treacherous waters of the Darien Gap, and smuggle it across the Panama-Colombia border.

Jesús was pleased. Back when they'd been moving drugs, he'd been the last guy in the chain—the one with all the risk. Now, with the weapons, he was the first rung on the ladder, and he liked it better this way.

"By the way," Jesús said casually as Ghost stood to leave, "stay away from the marketplace today. I hear there's gonna be trouble."

Ghost's spine stiffened. "What kind of trouble?"

Jesús shrugged. "Anti-U.S. protest, or something like that. Could get ugly."

Fuck. Becca!

Ghost muttered a quick goodbye and bolted out of the café, sprinting the whole way back toward the marketplace. Now that he knew what was coming, he could see it—small groups gathering in side streets, suspicious eyes scanning the square.

This was not going to end well.

Every combat-trained instinct in his body screamed at him. Trouble was brewing, and it was going to hit hard.

Frantically, he scanned the crowd outside the supermarket. Becca was standing at the edge of the square, a pile of carrier bags around her.

Thank God.

He switched directions and made a beeline for her, moving fast. As he passed a fruit stall, he saw a man lean in, whisper something to a woman who immediately dropped her shopping bag and bolted. That could only mean one thing.

"Becca, get down!" he roared.

Her head snapped up, eyes wide as she recognized his voice. "Mr. Dominguez, what's—"

Her words were cut off by the deafening blast that tore through the marketplace.

CHAPTER 6

*B*ecca hit the ground hard, but it wasn't just the explosion—it was the solid weight of Dominguez's body slamming into her, knocking the breath from her lungs.

She opened her mouth to scream, but the deafening blast swallowed her cry. The explosion was so loud it left her ears ringing, and she swore the ground trembled beneath her. Debris rained down, landing just feet away—wood, scraps of fabric, even a Panama hat spinning through the air.

Around them, people screamed, scattering like frightened birds. Chaos erupted all around, but she stayed frozen, too terrified to move.

Dominguez's body covered hers, shielding her from the fallout. His chest rose and fell, each heavy breath hot against her skin. His face was just inches from hers, and as their eyes locked, she saw more than concern in his intense gaze—something deeper, something that sent a different kind of shockwave through her.

"Are you okay?" he whispered, his voice gravelly, thick with adrenaline.

"I think so," she managed, though her pulse was still hammering in her ears. He smelled good, surprisingly—like clean soap, hot metal, and a hint of sunscreen. His weight pressed down on her, and despite the fear still buzzing in her veins, her body heated in places she didn't want to think about right now.

Get a grip, she told herself, but it didn't help. She could feel every inch of him, his hard muscles pinning her to the ground, his body hot against hers.

Wrong time, her brain insisted. But her body wasn't so sure.

She shifted slightly, trying to snap herself out of it, and he pushed up onto his elbows, his gaze still locked on hers.

"Sorry," he muttered, helping her sit up. "Let's get you on your feet."

With one strong tug, he pulled her upright. His hand, warm and solid around hers, lingered a little longer than necessary.

"You're sure you're okay? No headache? No dizziness?"

She shook her head, still feeling a little breathless—not from the blast, but from the way he was looking at her. His gaze was so gentle, so careful, like he was afraid she might shatter. It was nothing like the tough guy front he usually put on.

"Come on," he said quietly, his voice low and steady. "We need to get out of here. There might be a secondary explosion."

She let him lead her down a narrow side street, weaving through the panicked crowd as people fled the scene. Dominguez didn't let go of her hand, his grip firm and reassuring, guiding her like he knew exactly what he was doing.

They turned a corner and found themselves on a quieter road, far from the chaos of the market. They were in the heart of Panama City, surrounded by a blend of old and new buildings, but no one was stopping to admire the architecture now.

A few blocks later, they reached a small cantina, its brightly painted tables and chairs spilling out onto the sidewalk. The staff and customers were all on their feet, buzzing with nervous energy after hearing the explosion.

"Que pasó?" an elderly man asked, his weathered face creased with worry.

Becca didn't understand much Spanish, but she got the gist—he was asking what had happened.

Dominguez replied in a string of fluent Spanish, his voice low and authoritative.

Huh.

She hadn't expected him to speak the language so well, but with a name like Dominguez, she probably should have. It was one more layer to him she hadn't seen before.

The old man asked more questions, but Dominguez just shrugged and led her to an empty table. Only when she sat down did he finally let go of her hand.

"Thank you," she said softly, still catching her breath.

She looked at him, really looked at him, seeing the man behind the hard exterior. "I think you just saved my life."

He grinned, but there was an edge of humility to it. "I wouldn't go that far. Maybe I saved you from getting hit by a flying papaya."

She laughed, the sound shaky but genuine. The tension eased just a little. She dropped her hands into her lap, hoping he didn't notice how badly they were trembling. "I didn't see that coming," she admitted.

"Nobody did."

She studied him closely, her curiosity piqued. "You did." He had come running at her, shouting her name just before the blast. She was sure of it.

He didn't meet her gaze this time. "I saw the bomber give

a heads-up to some woman before she bolted. Didn't take a genius to figure out what was about to go down. You just know what to look for."

Was that all it was? she wondered. She still didn't know much about why he was here or who he was meeting. "Who would do something like that?"

"Anti-American group, probably," he said casually, picking up a menu like it was just another day.

Her hands were still shaking from the adrenaline, and she had this sudden urge to talk. "When I worked at the embassy, we were warned this kind of thing could happen. We did drills for it, but I never thought I'd actually be in one. When it's real, it's different. You freeze." She knew she was rambling, but the words kept spilling out. "I always wondered what I'd do in a moment like that, and now I know. I froze. I didn't move. I just stood there, waiting to get blown to bits."

"You're safe now," he said softly, waiting for her to catch her breath.

She stared at him for a long moment. There was something about the way he said it, something that made her feel like she really was safe with him. "You're used to this, though, right? Bombs going off around you?"

Before he could answer, her phone rang, breaking the tension. She fished it out of her bag, glancing at the screen.

"It's Ramirez," she mouthed to Dominguez, who shook his head, signaling her not to mention him.

She answered. "Yes, I'm okay," she said, keeping her voice steady. "No, I wasn't near it. I'll meet you in half an hour."

She hung up and turned to Dominguez. "Ramirez is coming to pick us up. We're meeting him a few blocks away to avoid the chaos."

In the distance, they could already hear the wail of sirens as police and ambulances rushed to the scene. The market was going to be crawling with officials and medics. She'd left her shopping, or what was left of it, back in the square. It was too bad.

"I hope no one was badly hurt," she whispered, biting her lip as the reality of what had just happened hit her. She'd come so close. If she'd been just a few feet closer to that stall...

"It was a powerful explosion, but it was controlled," he said. "The goal wasn't to kill. It was to send a message."

"How do you know that?" she asked, her heart still racing.

He gave her a half-smile, but it didn't reach his eyes. "Four tours in the Middle East. You get good at recognizing that kind of thing."

She couldn't help but be impressed.

Despite his messy hair and scruff, he was remarkably composed. His big, strong hands held the menu with steady ease, and he hadn't even broken a sweat. Meanwhile, she still felt shaky, her pulse erratic from the explosion—and maybe a little from his nearness.

His phone beeped. He pulled it from his pocket, glancing at the screen. She could have sworn he flinched, even if only for a second.

"That's my notification," he said, slipping it back.

Becca noticed the way he tensed up, his discomfort at being under Ramirez and Carlos's constant watch evident. She couldn't blame him—she wasn't a fan of their overbearing presence either.

"Why didn't you want Ramirez to know we were together?" she asked.

He gave a small shrug. "Didn't want to give him the wrong impression."

"What, that you're actually a nice guy?" She smirked, enjoying the way it made him squirm.

"Something like that." His grimace made her laugh.

She leaned in, dropping her voice into a teasing whisper. "Don't worry, your secret's safe with me. You can keep pretending to be the badass mercenary if it makes you feel better."

He chuckled, a low rumble in his chest that did weird things to her insides. "Thanks."

The waitress arrived, and Dominguez ordered for both of them, effortlessly taking control of the situation.

"I hope that has something strong in it," Becca sighed. "My nerves are shot."

"It's saco," he replied, his accent rolling easily. "You know it?"

She nodded. "I've heard of it but haven't tried it yet."

"It's local—distilled from sugarcane. It'll take the edge off."

She pursed her lips. "Right now, I'd drink anything, even tequila, and that's saying a lot."

He flashed her a grin, and for the first time, his eyes softened in the sunlight. She blinked. Was this Dominguez, the dangerous mercenary who looked like he could snap someone's neck with a flick of his wrist? How was it possible for him to have this... softer side?

Sitting across from him, it was hard to reconcile the two. She was so confused. This was the same man who had barreled into her like a human shield, protected her, held her hand all the way here... Where had the cold, calculating gun-for-hire gone?

Oh boy.

There she was again, making excuses for her attraction to a thoroughly unsuitable man. She'd sworn off bad boys—years ago, after a toxic relationship that had nearly broken her. Yet here she was, sitting across from one of the most dangerous men she'd ever met, feeling things she shouldn't be feeling.

She watched him as he lounged in his chair, deceptively relaxed. His sharp eyes, however, were still scanning their surroundings, taking everything in. He might look calm, but his body was coiled tight, ready for action at any moment. The contrast between his easy slouch and the tension in his muscles was captivating.

He caught her staring and smiled again, this time a little more knowingly.

Her stomach flipped, but she steeled herself.

No. Do not let your guard down.

Dominguez fit into this dangerous world. He belonged in it. If you stripped away the muscles and the dark, brooding eyes, he was still a guy with a gun, lethal as hell.

And nothing good ever came from getting involved with men like that.

She reached for her drink the moment it arrived and knocked it back in one gulp.

Dominguez's eyebrows lifted, amused. "It's not a soft drink, you know."

"I needed it," she shot back, setting down the empty glass. But not for the reason he thought.

"Want another?" he asked, though she noticed he hadn't touched his own drink yet.

She shook her head. "Just a bottle of water, please."

He flagged down the waitress again and ordered, all the while keeping his attention on her.

"Where did you learn to speak Spanish?" she asked. His command of the language was too good to be anything but native.

"I was born in Cuba," he replied, though his voice had a slight edge to it. Clearly, he didn't like talking about himself.

She frowned, confused. "I thought you were American. Your accent—"

"We moved to America when I was ten," he explained, eyes shadowed. "But we spoke Spanish at home."

Ah, that made sense.

The waitress brought her water, and Becca reached to twist off the cap but couldn't budge it. Her hands felt weak, the adrenaline crash hitting her hard.

Without a word, Dominguez took the bottle from her and opened it with a single twist of his wrist, handing it back.

"Thanks," she said, more softly than she intended. He'd done it again—this simple act of kindness, completely out of sync with the hard, violent image she'd built of him.

"You know," she said before she could stop herself, "I can't figure you out."

"How's that?" He took a sip of his saco, watching her carefully.

"Well, you're obviously good with a gun, or Mr. Markov wouldn't have hired you, which means you're dangerous. Carlos and Ramirez both respect you, and knowing them, that probably means you must have a reputation. Yet with me, you're... different. You protect me from explosions, carry my bag, open my water bottle." She shook her head. "You seem to be two people, Mr. Dominguez. Which one is the real you?"

He didn't answer right away, letting the sun beat down between them as he stared off into the distance. Then finally, his voice came low. "I'd like you to call me Dom."

Her heart skipped a beat. "Is that what your friends call you?"

"I don't have friends," he replied. "Not wise in my business."

Fair enough. She didn't have many either. Friends meant connections, especially to the past, and she didn't want to drag the past with her into her present.

"Well, Dom," she tested the name on her tongue. "Are you going to answer my question?"

He glanced away. "What was the question again?"

He was stalling, but she wasn't going to let him dodge it. "Who are you? The mercenary or the gentleman?"

His voice dropped to a low growl. "I don't think you want me to answer that."

A thrill raced up her spine that had nothing to do with the alcohol working its way into her system. *So he's a bit of both.*

She took another sip of water, trying to steady herself.

"How much do you know about your boss's business?" he asked, his voice tighter now.

She gave the rehearsed answer, the official line. "He sells farming equipment."

"That's what he told you?"

"Well, it's true, isn't it?" she challenged, lifting her chin. If he wanted to dig deeper, it would force him to admit the truth about what he was really doing here.

He shrugged, noncommittal. "I guess so."

She sighed, deciding to level with him. "It's not the whole truth though, is it? Otherwise, why would he need someone like you?"

His jaw clenched, but his voice softened. "I'm not just a hired gun, Becca. I spent fifteen years in the Marine Corps. I've earned the right to call myself a soldier."

"I know."

His eyes narrowed. "How do you know?"

She kept her voice steady. "I did a background check on you. Standard protocol."

His expression darkened, but before he could speak, the waitress returned, asking if they wanted anything else. He shook his head, dismissing her.

"What else did you find out?" he asked, his tone edging into something more dangerous.

She saw the tension in his jaw, the muscles flexing in his forearms, tight beneath that faded T-shirt.

God, those arms.

Her eyes flicked back to his face. "You joined the Marine Corps at seventeen, then went into special operations after ten years. You specialized in close combat and jungle survival." She gestured around them. "I guess Panama must feel pretty familiar to you."

"I trained in the jungles of Central America," he muttered, as if that explained it all.

She leaned in a little. "What I want to know is, why did you go AWOL?"

"Enough about me." His tone sharpened as he drained his drink, deftly avoiding the question. "Let's talk about you."

Becca raised an eyebrow. "There's nothing to talk about. My life's pretty boring."

He gave her a long, appraising look. "Come on, that's not fair. I haven't had the benefit of a background check. The least you could do is fill me in on the basics."

She sighed, resigned. "Okay, here goes. I grew up in North Carolina with my mom. Pretty standard upbringing. But when she passed, I went off the rails for a bit. Moved to Cali for a while." She paused, then added, "It didn't go well, so I moved to Europe. Lived in Paris for a couple of months, then Amsterdam, then Prague. Eventually came home."

"How old were you when she died?"

"Eighteen. It messed me up for a while—we were very close."

"What about your father? Where was he?"

She hesitated. "I never knew him growing up."

"I'm sorry. My mother passed away when I was a kid, but I don't remember much about her."

"I recall reading that in your file," she said softly. "It couldn't have been easy, growing up without a mom."

He shrugged. "My father did the best he could." His eyes clouded over, but when he looked at her again, they cleared. "How did you end up here?"

"Oh, well, that's another story." She fast-forwarded ten years. "I went to Costa Rica on a surf trip." *With this guy...* "And while I was there, I spotted the advert for the job at the American Embassy in Panama." It had been time to move on.

"That's where Markov found you," Dom finished.

She glanced up in surprise. "He tell you that?"

Dom nodded. "Said he stole you from them."

She tilted her head to the side. "You could say that. He was very persuasive." She didn't elaborate, but she didn't need to—he got the picture.

"You're a bit of a gypsy, aren't you?" he remarked, taking out his wallet.

"Please, let me." She reached into her bag, but he waved her away.

"I've got this."

She smiled her thanks. He was full of surprises.

"I guess so. I haven't found anywhere to settle down yet, but I hope to one day."

Or anyone to settle down with.

To be honest, she wasn't sure she was the settling down type. She'd been bouncing around for so long it had become a way of life. When things got stale, she moved on. When things got serious, she moved on. Maybe she was a gypsy, after all.

He stood, easing to his feet like a lithe panther. She tried to do the same, but she was stiff from her fall, and her shoulder ached where he'd barreled into her.

"You okay?" he asked as she grimaced. He didn't miss a thing.

"I'm fine." She draped her bag over her good shoulder, and they started walking back up the road.

"Here, let me take that for you," he offered, removing the bag from her shoulder. It wasn't heavy, and she was about to resist when he sent her a "don't argue" look.

So, she shut her mouth and let him carry it.

"What's it like working for Markov?" he asked.

She watched the cracks in the road as they walked. "It's fine. I like the job. The estate's beautiful, more like a resort, and I pretty much do things my way. No one's looking over my shoulder like they did at the embassy. Alek only cares if things run smoothly."

Dom glanced at her. "For what it's worth, he was singing your praises."

She smiled. "Good to know."

"And you're cool working for a guy without knowing what he's really up to?"

They gave the market a wide berth, taking a street that ran parallel to it. Sirens and loud voices still echoed in the distance. They were only a block from the pickup point.

"It's better that way," she said. Why was he so hung up about that? Who she worked for had nothing to do with him. It wasn't like he was a paragon of virtue.

"It doesn't seem to bother you," she blurted out.

He stared straight ahead. "There's not a lot of work for guys like me. I take what I can get, and Markov pays well."

"Really? I thought that in this part of the world, there was a lot of work for a good gunslinger."

He didn't reply.

CHAPTER 7

Ghost led the way to the pickup point. Carlos would be here any moment. It was a busy street and the traffic whizzed by in a motion blur. He could feel the heat of the engines on his legs.

"Becca." He turned to face her.

She glanced up at him. "Yes?"

"Your bag." He suddenly remembered he was still carrying it.

She took it with a little nod. "Thanks."

He hesitated. Today had not gone according to plan. The explosion had thrown him off kilter, but at the same time, it had given him the perfect opportunity to take her for a drink. But being alone with her, getting to know her, had given him something else to worry about.

Her.

She was in way over her head. Either she had no idea what Markov was up to, in which case she was unknowingly putting herself at risk, or she did know, and she was in danger of being dragged down with him when the shit hit the fan.

She was still looking at him, her head tilted to the side. Waiting for him to say something. Sensing that he had something to say.

Spit it out, man.

"Hey, Becca. I just want you to know... If anything happens to you, or you need my help, you just have to call." Now he wished he could take it back. She was staring at him like he'd declared his undying love for her.

"Why do you think something's going to happen to me?" she whispered. Fear tickled the edges of her eyes.

When he didn't immediately reply, she said, "Dom, is something going to happen?"

He averted his gaze. "No, of course not."

Yes. Eventually.

When we take down your crooked boss.

He tried to brush it off. "It's just in case, that's all. This isn't the safest country in the world, and we live in a complex surrounded by armed guards. I wanted you to know you could count on me."

"Like you took care of me today?" Her voice was soft.

The way she was looking at him made him want to kiss her so bad it hurt. His gaze dropped to her lips. "I did what anyone in my position would have done."

She moved closer to him, and his heart skipped a beat. "I think you went way beyond what a gun for hire would do."

His breath caught in his throat. Those eyes. Those lips. He was about to lift his hand to her face when Markov's black SUV with Carlos in the passenger seat swooped down the street.

She hurriedly stepped back.

"I haven't got your number," she whispered, as reality came to a halt beside them and Carlos gestured for them to get in.

"I've got yours," he murmured, before opening the back door for her. "I'll call you tonight, then you'll have mine."

"Okay." She climbed into the car.

He got in beside her.

This time they sat a little closer together than they had on the way here. Along with her intoxicating scent, he could feel the heat from her body. Her legs were crossed towards his and her arm was only an inch or so away, resting on the canvas bag she'd placed between them. The car turned a corner causing her to tilt over and her arm touched his. She turned and smiled at him. He smiled back.

This hadn't been the plan, but something was happening here. He'd won her trust, that was a big step forward. The problem was, he very much feared he might be losing something in the process, something he couldn't afford to give away.

His heart.

BACK AT THE HACIENDA, Ghost sat on his deck in the late afternoon sun and thought about Becca.

What did she mean when she'd said she'd gone off the rails? You wouldn't think it to look at her. With those sharp features, those deep, honey-colored eyes, and her cool, efficient manner, she seemed born to be an executive assistant. So damn organized and put-together, it was hard to imagine her as some restless gypsy who wandered the world and couldn't settle down—or the young woman who'd gone off the rails in Europe.

Yet here she was, working for one of the biggest crooks in Latin America. Maybe she was a danger junkie. She had to know the risks, but by her own admission, she was willfully ignoring what Markov was up to.

He wondered if Pat had dug up any intel on her.

At least Markov wasn't screwing her. Ghost was sure of that. Not that he should care, but somehow, he did. The arms dealer's wife and mistress probably kept him busy enough. Still, the thought gnawed at him—what if Markov made a move?

Would Becca be able to say no?

A rejection like that would bruise Markov's ego, and bruises like that usually led to one thing: getting rid of the problem. Ghost scowled at the horizon, then got up to grab another beer.

He hadn't missed how Markov watched her. The guy might not want her in his bed, but he still *owned* her, and he made sure she knew it. Like the way she had to ask permission before heading into town. She called him *Alek* earlier, too. Ghost could see the writing on the wall. Markov was twice her age, but he'd make his move eventually.

Ghost pulled out his burner—the one Markov had the number for, along with his contacts and now Becca. His *other* phone, the one he used to contact Pat, stayed hidden in a secret compartment in his backpack. No numbers saved on it. Calls were quick and dirty—straight to the point, then deleted. Nobody had found that one.

He ignored the strange twist in his gut and called her. It rang a few times before she picked up.

"Hello?"

"It's Mr. Dominguez," he said, keeping it formal. Just in case anyone was listening.

"Hi." She sounded breathless. "What can I do for you?"

There was an awkward pause that made him feel like a high school kid calling a girl for the first time. He cleared his throat. "You said to call if I needed anything."

"What do you need, Mr. Dominguez?" She was playing along. That confirmed what he thought, that their calls might be monitored.

"Some fresh towels."

"Sure, I'll have someone bring them down."

He hung up. The shortness of the call might raise a brow, but he had to stick to his cover. A hired gun didn't waste time on small talk.

When they'd been together, he'd been himself, —or mostly himself—so she could see what he was really like. He wasn't going to win her over if he acted like a prick. But for the sake of the mission, and any listening ears, he had to keep up appearances.

The sun was still hot, so he hit the water for a quick swim. The ocean was refreshing and helped cool more than his overheated skin.

Twenty minutes later, back on the deck, he spotted Becca walking down the path toward his cabin, towels in hand, the sun catching in her hair. He was at the door by the time she got there.

"You came yourself?"

"Maria has left for the day." Her gaze dipped to his bare chest and stayed there a second too long.

He'd seen the woman cleaning earlier, a local from the nearby village. The woman, like most of the casual staff, didn't know what Markov did. Hell, she probably thought she was cleaning for some rich businessman, which is how she could come and go with just a light search at the gates.

Anyone in the know got the bag treatment, with an escort.

"Thanks. Come in." He stepped back, letting her pass.

She'd changed out of the skirt and blouse and was now in a flowing, white cotton dress, buttons running all the way down the front. It floated around her, barely touching her skin, and Ghost felt a wave of heat wash over him.

"Can I get you a drink?" His voice came out rougher than he intended. "I don't have much—just beer."

She set the towels down and faced him. "I don't think that's a good idea." But her eyes said something different.

He stepped closer, catching that soft scent again, the one that messed with his head. "Didn't stop you before. You knocked back that saco like a pro."

She grinned. "That was in town, and I had a good excuse. My nerves were fried from the explosion. This is different. My boss would kill me if he knew I was fraternizing with his *associates*."

"*Associates*?" He smirked. "I thought I was a dangerous mercenary."

She smiled back. "Even worse."

He forced himself to stop grinning like a fool and touched her arm. "Come on, just one drink. I won't tell if you don't."

She hesitated, then took a step back. "Fine, just one."

Had she also felt that jolt of electricity that had passed between them?

"And beer's fine."

She walked out onto the deck while he grabbed a couple from the fridge.

"Beautiful, isn't it?" she said when he joined her. The sun was starting to sink, painting the sky with streaks of pink and gold. He handed her a beer, his eyes tracing the way the light danced off her skin, her hair, her eyes.

"Yeah, it is." His voice came out low, his gaze locked on her.

She didn't notice. "Could be in a damn travel brochure."

He glanced at the horizon, forcing his eyes off her. "It's perfect for photographs."

She gave him a curious look. "You're a photographer too? Another one of Dom's hidden talents?"

He shrugged. "A bit. I've got a camera, but I don't carry anything fancy. It'd get wrecked where I go."

"Where's that?"

"The jungle, mostly." He didn't elaborate. "After I got kicked out of Special Forces, I thought about photography, but other opportunities came up. Besides, it's better as a hobby. If it was a job, it'd lose the appeal."

"What other opportunities?" she asked, leaning back against the railing.

"The training facility. But then, like you, I got poached."

"By the bad guys?"

He smirked. "You could say that. But they pay well."

"They always do." She studied him a moment, then said, "Guess we've got more in common than I thought. We're both easily led astray."

His eyes locked on hers. Photography would've been the safer option. "I was trained for this. You weren't."

"I did a secretarial course." Her eyes twinkled.

He snorted. "Not what I meant."

"I know, but I'm safe here as long as I do my job and stay out of Mr. Markov's business. And he pays me a hell of a lot more than I got at the embassy. When I leave, I'll be able to afford a place of my own. Start fresh."

"Is that what you want? A fresh start?"

Her gaze drifted out to the horizon. "Yeah. I think it's time I put down some roots. I've been bouncing around too long."

"I thought you liked the gypsy life."

She frowned. "It's complicated."

"It always is."

He raised his beer, taking a long drink.

They watched as the sun dipped below the treeline.

A short time later she said, "I should get back before it's dark—or someone notices I'm not there."

"I can walk you."

"That's okay."

He followed her to the door. That scent—magnolia and

something softer—wrapped around him. She hesitated before stepping out.

"Is it drugs or weapons?" she asked quietly, her eyes searching his. "Or both?"

"Weapons," he said after a pause.

"From Eastern Europe?"

"Probably."

"And you smuggle them across the border for him?"

He nodded.

Her eyes narrowed, like she was trying to read him. "So, you're an arms trafficker, mercenary, and soldier." It wasn't really a question.

He didn't respond. She wasn't wrong.

She reached out, her hand resting on his chest, and he sucked in a breath.

Shit.

"Yet tonight, you're still the gentleman. Or is that just for me?"

She was sharp, he'd give her that. The truth was, he *was* into her. Badly. All he wanted was to pick her up, carry her upstairs, and peel that dress off one button at a time.

Damn.

He was losing it.

Somehow, he managed to keep his cool. "What can I say? You bring out the best in me."

She smiled. "That's a new one." Her fingers traced up his chest, her breath catching like she was waiting for something to break.

And break it did.

The tension coiled tight inside him snapped, and he cupped her neck, pulling her into a kiss.

CHAPTER 8

Becca felt Dom's lips crush down on hers, and everything inside her melted.

Hell yes.

She'd started this, sure, but the way he'd been looking at her—like she was the cream on top of his favorite dessert—had set something off inside her. She *wanted* to be that cream.

Her heart pounded as she clutched at his smooth, hard shoulders. Ever since he'd thrown himself over her in the marketplace, shielding her from the blast, she hadn't been able to stop thinking about him. Was that wrong?

Maybe it was some primal need to feel protected, or maybe it was just because it had been so damn long since she'd been touched by a man. Either way, she wasn't pulling back now.

She opened her mouth, inviting him in, and let out a low moan as their tongues met. He didn't just kiss—he *claimed* her, tasted her, and she felt it all the way down to her toes. Her whole body responded, letting him explore her mouth so intimately it almost felt indecent.

Delicious. Irresistible.

She clung to him, fingers digging into his shoulders as his rock-solid chest pressed against hers, his hands gripping her waist like he couldn't let go. The aggression in his kiss, mixed with a tenderness that took her breath away, lit her up inside.

He smelled good, too—like sun and sea, with a faint trace of beer on his breath. Needing more, she stretched up on her tiptoes, hands winding around his neck, feeling the tickle of his hair against her arms.

More.

She pressed herself against him, not giving a damn what he thought.

Dom matched her intensity, stepping forward and pinning her against the wall. They were all over each other, and Becca was grateful for the cool slats at her back, because every inch of her was burning where his hard, ripped body crushed against hers. She held on tight, legs barely holding her up.

Then his hands moved, cupping her ass, lifting her, and sending a shockwave straight through her core. She gasped as the solid length of him pressed into her.

Sweet baby cheeses.

Pinned between him and the wall, she could feel his heartbeat pounding against her—or maybe that was hers. It didn't matter. They were pressed together, moving as one, their need tangled up in a messy, hungry knot.

There was nothing gentlemanly about him now. His stubble scraped her chin as he devoured her, and his thigh slipped between her legs, forcing them apart. Her body betrayed her, grinding against him, a groan escaping her lips as she tangled her fingers in his thick hair.

He was breathing hard, his hips moving slow and deliberate against her, his hands gripping her ass tighter, pulling her closer.

Oh, God. She was a trembling, slick mess, barely holding

it together. It was a miracle she didn't fall apart right there. Just when she thought she might lose it completely, he broke away, gasping for breath.

"Dom," she whispered, staring at him, her mind still spinning.

What the *hell* just happened?

He slowly let her down, her back sliding against the wall until her feet found the ground again. His chest rose and fell with heavy breaths, and his eyes were dark with something raw, something that made her feel like she was standing on the edge of a cliff.

"Becca, I..." He didn't finish.

No words needed.

"I know." She breathed out, trying to steady herself, running a shaky hand through her hair. She was still buzzing with adrenaline, with need—hell, with *shock*. That was more intense than anything she'd ever felt before.

Dom shut his eyes, like he was cutting himself off. "You'd better go before you're missed."

She swallowed hard, reaching for the door, her pulse still racing. He was right. She needed to go, but not because she was worried about being missed. She needed to leave because if she didn't, she wasn't sure she'd ever find the strength to walk out.

But Dom didn't try to stop her as she slipped out the door and stumbled down the stairs into the clearing.

Run, the voice in her head screamed. *Run while you still can.*

Refusing to look back, she quickened her pace, breaking into a full sprint down the overgrown path toward the house.

BECCA WAS STILL SHAKING by the time she got back. Running into Carlos hadn't helped. He'd been standing by the pool, watching the terrace, and had seen her emerge from the path leading to Dom's cabin.

"It's late for a walk," he said, his eyes sweeping over her, taking in her messy appearance.

"I like it when it's cooler," she replied, struggling to keep her voice even.

He narrowed his eyes but didn't say more, just stood there watching as she hurried past, heading to her apartment through the garden.

Shit, that was close.

She was going to have to be more careful. Then she shook her head. What the hell was she thinking? Of course, she wasn't going to visit Dom again. There *wasn't* going to be a next time. That'd be insane.

She collapsed onto the couch in her small living room, heart still pounding. One, her boss would lose his mind if he ever found out, and two, she didn't need that kind of trouble in her life.

Not that kind of trouble. Dangerous. Destructive. Addictive.

Stop.

Hadn't she learned her lesson years ago? This was why she hadn't let herself get close to anyone for the last decade. No strings, no ties, no commitment, no liabilities. Keep it simple.

Not that Dom was offering any of those things, but it wasn't *him* she was scared of—it was herself. Being in his arms had felt so right, too right. Like she belonged there. Did he feel it too? It was strange, feeling that kind of protection from someone like him—a man who made his living dealing in violence.

Her phone buzzed on the coffee table. She glanced down, her stomach flipping at the thought that it might be him.

What if it *was*? Would she go back?

No way. She couldn't. She wouldn't.

She exhaled when she saw it was only Chrissy, Ramirez's wife. Maybe she'd heard about the explosion and was checking in.

"Chrissy, how are you?" she answered, trying to keep her voice light.

What greeted her wasn't relief, but sobbing.

Becca's heart sank. "Chrissy, take a breath. I can't understand you. What's wrong?"

"He's having an affair," Chrissy blurted between sobs.

Becca winced. *Of course he is.* Ramirez had never struck her as a faithful husband.

"He's screwing the au pair," Chrissy spat, then laughed bitterly. "How *typical*."

The au pair. Becca groaned inwardly. The poor girl had been picking up the kids from boarding school on Fridays, bringing them home for the weekend. Clearly, she'd been offering *extra* services lately.

"How'd you find out?" Becca asked, knowing this was going to be bad.

"She was acting different around him. You know, that stupid, secretive way you get when you're in love but trying to hide it. So, I confronted her. She confessed, so I fired her."

Of course you did, Becca thought.

"What about Ramirez? Did you talk to him?"

"I did." The venom in Chrissy's voice was palpable. "He said if I left him, he'd take the girls. Said I'd never see them again."

Her voice broke again into tears. "He threatened me, Becca."

Becca clenched her jaw. Of course he did. Ramirez had the money, the power, and in cases like this, that's all it took to hold someone's life in a chokehold. Chrissy had nothing of her own, no leverage. Everything was tied to him. It was why

Becca had never let herself get trapped like that. It was too easy to lose yourself.

"Do you want to get together and talk it over?" Becca offered. "You could come by tomorrow."

"I'm not coming near that place," Chrissy hissed, her words slurred from booze. "It's *your* fucking boss who put him up to this. Alek Markov is a bastard."

Becca grimaced. That wasn't hard to believe. Whether it was Markov's advice, his shady lawyers, or just the general aura of power he exuded, Chrissy wasn't wrong. Markov wasn't exactly a shining example of virtue.

"I *know* things," Chrissy's voice dropped to a whisper. "He thinks I don't, but I do."

Becca sat up straighter. "What things, Chrissy?"

"I'm not as dumb as I look. If he knew what I'd done…" Her laugh was bitter, broken.

Becca's pulse picked up. What the hell had she done?

"Listen, Chrissy, let's meet up and—"

"Like that's gonna help."

Becca sighed. "Okay. But I'm here if you need to talk."

"How can you *stand* it?" Chrissy wailed. "How can you work for him? You're just as trapped as I am, Becca. He's got you right where he wants you. Just like Ramirez has me."

The line went dead.

Becca let the phone drop onto the couch, rubbing her hands over her face. Chrissy was more than drunk; she was a wreck. Who could blame her? Her husband was cheating, her marriage was crumbling, and she could lose her kids.

Poor Chrissy.

Becca shook her head. There wasn't much she could do for her except be a shoulder to cry on. Ramirez was a prick. After Markov, she hadn't met anyone more ruthless, ambitious, or self-serving. Chrissy must've known what she was getting into when she married him. The real surprise was that they'd lasted this long. Their girls were teenagers already.

But who was she to judge? Maybe Chrissy, like her, was just drawn to the wrong kind of man.

She headed for the shower, hoping to wash off the heavy weight of the phone call. But even when she stepped out, her skin flushed pink and shiny, she didn't feel any cleaner.

Chrissy's situation hit closer than she'd expected. That's what happens when you tie your life to someone else's. When you hand over your freedom. You're stuck with them, for better or worse. Sure, Chrissy could leave, but at what cost? Lose her kids? Or stay in a loveless marriage with a man she despised?

Becca shivered despite the warm night air. Was that what was in store for her? A life tied to someone who saw her as property?

Her thoughts drifted to Dom. His lips. His hands on her, gripping her, lifting her. She let out a long breath.

That kiss—hell, that whole moment—had to be the first and *last* time. She deserved more than a fling with a gun-running merc. Even if he was an insanely good kisser.

One more year. She could make it that long. And then she'd leave. Markov would understand—hell, he'd probably expect it. She'd hand in her notice and get the hell out of there.

Somewhere new. Somewhere she could start fresh.

Somewhere she could finally be *free*.

CHAPTER 9

Things were moving fast—*too* fast.

Markov had gotten confirmation from the Colombians, and the full-scale shipment was greenlit. Half the money up-front, the rest on delivery. It was happening. The deal was locked in, and soon, one of the deadliest cartels in Colombia would be swimming in enough firepower to take on half the country.

Ghost had already been handed his cut—just enough to cover "operating expenses"—which he'd passed on to his distributors. He was playing along, setting everything up like he was supposed to, but the truth gnawed at him. After this deal, he'd be complicit in arming a cartel that made most drug lords look like amateurs.

The upside? He was close—*so close*—to getting Markov to reveal his cache of weapons. If he could pinpoint the location, the authorities could step in, seize whatever was left, or burn it to the ground. It wouldn't stop the shipment, but it'd slow Markov down, cripple him.

That's why he was here now, waiting outside Markov's office, trying not to look like he was about to head out on a mission that could get him killed. He'd be gone for days, accompanying the shipment to the border, making sure everything went smooth. The Colombians didn't tolerate mistakes, and if there was one thing Markov was afraid of, it was the cartels. They made his strong-arm tactics look like a charity mission.

Then Becca walked in.

They hadn't spoken since that kiss.

That. Kiss.

And holy hell, it still hit him like a truck.

He'd been avoiding her—*had* to—but apparently, she'd been doing the same. Their paths hadn't crossed once in three days, and he knew she was keeping her distance.

But seeing her now? It was like a punch to the gut.

She looked incredible—dark hair glossy as ever, swishing with each step. That skirt? It was straight-up *designed* to mess with his head, hugging her curves in all the right places. And the silk blouse, just sheer enough to hint at the soft curve of her breasts, wasn't doing him any favors either. He had to force himself to keep it together.

A sudden, irrational urge to stride across the office, pull her into his arms, and kiss the hell out of her hit him so hard he almost moved.

Almost.

He wasn't into suicide.

"Good morning, Mr. Dominguez," she said, in a polite, no-nonsense tone. The kind of voice that gave nothing away.

He nodded, fighting to keep his expression neutral, but his mind was racing. He wanted to talk to her. Hell, he *needed* her help if he was going to pull this off. She was the only one with access to the right information, and without her, he was flying blind.

But then Ramirez walked in behind her.

Fuck.

Any chance of talking to her now was gone.

He swallowed the frustration burning in his gut. Pat had made it clear—unless he could get Markov to the final drop, they needed something solid. Hard evidence tying him to the cartels. An invoice, a payment record, anything. Something that'd hold up in front of a judge and put Markov away for good.

Otherwise, Ghost's whole mission would go up in smoke, and worse, the U.S. government would have blood on its hands for letting a known arms dealer move weapons across the border.

He couldn't let that happen.

Jesus and his brother were already lined up, ready to move the crates from the warehouse to the rendezvous point on the city's outskirts. From there, it'd be a slick handoff to the loggers, who'd haul the goods deep into the jungle. After that, the shipment would disappear onto a fisherman's boat, skimming across the border through those swampy, winding rivers only he knew like the back of his hand. Once the weapons hit Colombian soil, it was all up to Miguel and his crew.

Ramirez's phone rang, loud and sharp. He grunted and stepped outside to answer, leaving him alone with Becca.

Finally.

"We need to talk," he hissed, keeping his voice low.

Becca's eyes darted to the door where Ramirez was barking into his phone. "When?"

"Can you meet me later?" He tried to keep his voice steady, but it wasn't easy. He *needed* her to say yes.

She hesitated, biting her lip, then whispered, "I don't know. Carlos saw me coming back from your cabin the other night. I think he's watching me."

Shit. That explained the radio silence. Carlos was a snake, always lurking in the shadows. If he suspected anything, this whole thing could blow up in their faces.

"Okay, I'll come to you," he said, eyes scanning the room.

Her eyes widened with worry. "There are cameras everywhere."

"Don't worry," he said. "I know where they are."

She opened her mouth to respond, but Ramirez barged back in, phone in hand. "Ready?" he grunted, looking at Ghost.

He clenched his jaw. "Yeah."

Ramirez knocked on Markov's door, and a moment later, they were both ushered inside, leaving Becca behind in the outer office. Ghost could feel her eyes on his back as the door closed.

This was it.

Everything hinged on the next few days. If he didn't find that weapons cache, Markov would slip through their fingers, and the U.S. Government would have directly armed the cartel.

He had no choice but to trust Becca.

He just had to hope she was brave enough to trust him back.

CHAPTER 10

There was a culinary crisis in the kitchen, so Becca didn't see Dom leave. The spoiled lamb had derailed the dinner plans, and now, the staff were scrambling to come up with a last-minute alternative. As she darted back and forth between the kitchen and the storeroom, her mind wandered back to *him*.

Tonight. He'd come tonight.

A delicious shiver ran down her spine. It had been three days since she'd seen him—three long days of thinking about wrapping herself around that hard, chiseled body and giving in to the desire that simmered just beneath the surface. But that's all it was. A dream. A tantalizing, forbidden fantasy she could never act on again.

Never.

Dom was bad news. Guns, blurred lines, danger. The trifecta of everything she'd sworn to avoid. He ticked every single one of those boxes with a big, fat, permanent marker.

But damn it, that didn't make it any easier to stay away. She sighed, knowing she was in trouble. She was falling for him, and there was no use denying it anymore. The first step to healing is admitting you have a problem, right? Well, there it was. Dom was her problem. One she couldn't afford to have.

The spoiled lamb had to be replaced with something quick, so she gave orders to the staff to whip up a batch of fresh seafood from the stockpile. Markov wouldn't tolerate anything less than a perfect meal, and they were already on thin ice after last week's fiasco.

Ramirez, however, was an easier mark. He made it a habit to eat at the villa most nights, despite whatever drama was brewing at home. Becca kept a room ready for him, knowing full well that his overnights were usually triggered by a fight with his wife or an overdose of wine at dinner. The villa had become his second home.

Becca dealt with the crisis, issuing instructions to the staff and checking the final arrangements for the new menu. But as she made her way back towards Markov's study, she saw Carlos sprinting past her, a rare sight. Carlos didn't run unless something serious was happening. A knot formed in her stomach.

From behind the study door, she could hear raised voices—Markov, Ramirez, and Carlos, all shouting over one another. Becca hesitated just outside, her hand hovering over the doorknob, torn between curiosity and the fear of getting caught eavesdropping.

Before she could decide, the door flew open, and Ramirez stormed out, fury etched into every line of his face.

Becca watched from the window as he marched around the back of the villa, straight to his armored Mercedes. He was in a rage, practically vibrating with anger as he climbed inside, slamming the door so hard it made her flinch. A second later, he tore down the driveway, tires squealing.

What the hell just happened?

Unable to resist, she pushed open Markov's office door. "What's going on?" she asked, stepping inside cautiously.

Her boss was pacing, his expression tight with frustration. "The stupid bastard," he muttered under his breath, shaking his head. Becca had never seen him so rattled. She turned toward Carlos, who stood near the window, staring after Ramirez with an inscrutable look on his face.

"Alek?" she pressed, her voice softer now.

Markov stopped pacing and turned to face her, his eyes dark with something close to regret. "Brace yourself," he said, his voice gruff. "Chrissy was killed in a car accident. It happened about an hour ago."

The words hit her like a punch to the gut.

"Oh my God," she whispered, her legs giving out as she collapsed into the nearest chair.

Chrissy, dead?

It didn't seem possible. She'd just spoken to her just last night—heard her laugh, listened to her vent about Ramirez.

Now, she was gone?

Becca's mind reeled, struggling to keep up with the shock.

"Are they sure it's her?" Becca asked, clinging to a thread of hope. "The au pair sometimes drives her car. Maybe it wasn't Chrissy—"

Markov cut her off with a grim nod. "It's her. Ramirez spoke to the au pair. She's gone to collect the girls from school. He's on his way there now to break the news."

"Those poor kids," Becca murmured, her voice hollow.

What the hell had happened?

First, the affair. Now this. It was too much, too fast.

"How... how did it happen?"

"I don't have all the details yet," Markov barked, clearly hating the uncertainty. He was a man who thrived on control, and this was beyond him. "When I do, I'll let you know."

Becca rose to her feet, her limbs shaky. That was her cue to leave, to give them space to handle the fallout. As she walked towards the door, she couldn't shake the words that Markov had muttered when she entered. *"The stupid bastard."*

What the hell did that mean?

A flicker of suspicion darted through her mind, but she pushed it aside. Ramirez wouldn't have... not Chrissy. He had his faults—plenty of them—but he wouldn't do something like that. Would he?

She closed the door behind her and collapsed into her desk chair, her hands trembling. Chrissy. Dead. It was surreal. The woman had been a wreck the night before—drunk, angry, spiraling—but dead? She hadn't sounded *that* far gone.

Becca's mind raced, conjuring up images of Chrissy, red-eyed and reckless, behind the wheel of her car. Had she been drinking? Driving erratically in a fit of rage? The pieces were scattered, but no matter how hard Becca tried to force them into place, the picture didn't make sense.

Then there was Markov. His cold, businesslike demeanor told her everything she needed to know about where his priorities lay. Chrissy's death didn't affect him personally—it was all about Ramirez. His long-time associate would either be more useful or more volatile after this. It was all about calculating the next move, keeping everything smooth for the business.

Becca sat at her desk for a long time, staring into space as the weight of it all pressed down on her. Ramirez's wife, a friend—*gone*. And those girls. Their lives had just been shattered.

After a while, Carlos slinked out of the study, his usual leering glance absent. He stalked past her without a word, and not long after, Markov left the villa as well. Probably headed to Adriana's place. He hadn't spent much time with his girlfriend since Dom had arrived and this business with the Colombians had ramped up.

The villa was eerily quiet now, and for the first time, Becca allowed herself to cry. Silent tears slid down her cheeks, her chest tight with the weight of the loss. She hadn't been *that* close to Chrissy, but she'd been a friend. A mom. And now, two teenage girls would grow up without their mother.

The thought made her stomach churn. Ramirez wasn't exactly parent material, and with Chrissy gone, Becca didn't doubt for a second that the au pair would take her place—whether she wanted to or not.

God, she hoped she was wrong.

But the more she thought about it, the more suspicious it all seemed. Chrissy had been angry, sure, but running a red light in a fit of rage? Something didn't sit right. Unable to shake the feeling, she picked up the phone and called an old contact from the American embassy.

"Hi, Robert, it's Becca. Long time, huh?" she said, keeping her voice light, despite the nerves gnawing at her. After a few minutes of catching up, she got to the point. "I was hoping you could help me with something."

She filled him in on what she needed, and Robert promised to look into it. He had connections with the local authorities and could access police reports when necessary. Becca knew she could trust him to find out what happened.

She tried to focus on work after the call, but her mind was spinning. Eventually, she gave up and headed back to her apartment, where she let the emotions wash over her in a long, hot bath.

Chrissy had sounded desperate last night. Desperate enough to do something reckless. Maybe she *had* driven too fast, blinded by anger. Maybe it really was nothing more than a tragic accident.

She was drying off when her phone rang again.

Robert.

"Hey, Rob. What did you find out?"

"Well, Becca, it looks like an accident on paper. Your friend ran a red light, and a truck hit her broadside. She didn't stand a chance."

Becca's heart sank. "Was she drinking?"

"She had a blood alcohol level well above the legal limit," Robert confirmed. "It's pretty cut and dry."

Becca nodded, even though he couldn't see her. *That explained it then.*

But Robert paused.

"There is something else, though. I don't know if it's relevant, but she was booked on a flight out to LAX tonight. Three seats."

Becca's blood ran cold. *Chrissy had been running.*

CHAPTER 11

It was pitch black in the natural forest behind Ghost's cabin. The sky had settled into an inky indigo, stars swallowed by thick clouds, the sounds of the jungle humming around him. He stood still, eyes scanning the tangled mess of trees and plants, thick vines knitting together so tightly no light could pierce through. This was where the jungle hit the beach, the wilderness eventually giving way to the soft sand of the coast.

The light in his cabin was still on. A small decoy to keep the guards convinced he was safely holed up for the night. He was supposed to be tucked away, keeping a low profile, but he had other plans. He'd only taken what he needed—a flashlight, his lock-picking set, and his army knife, the one Carlos had missed during their last pat-down.

He melted into the bushes, blending into the shadows. The undergrowth was thick and knotted, but Ghost knew better than to let it slow him down. The jungle was his terrain. He could move through it like a wraith, slipping under branches and over twisted roots without a sound. He'd learned the rhythm of the forest long ago. Now, even the cicadas buzzing in the night made more noise than him.

Twenty minutes in, he spotted a flicker of light. He was close. Becca's apartment wasn't far—tucked into the eastern wing of the villa, away from the guards who congregated near the pool, smoking and swapping stories during their rounds. He stayed low, darting from tree cover to the shadow of a bougainvillea bush. His black clothes and balaclava kept him invisible under the cloak of night.

Becca's patio door was just ahead, locked, of course, but not enough of a deterrent to stop him. Ghost crouched in the shadows, assessing the two cameras positioned on the terrace. Both were pointed away from where he stood, leaving a blind spot along the eastern wall. It was a flaw he'd noticed early on. Markov's men didn't seem to care about the details, and that suited him just fine.

Sticking to the cover of the bougainvillea, he moved to the patio door, the lock-picking set sliding into his hand like an extension of his body. Within seconds, the door clicked open. He slipped inside, closing the wooden door behind him without a sound. His senses went on high alert, waiting for footsteps, a sign that he'd tripped something—but there was nothing. Just the soft hum of the villa settling for the night.

He exhaled quietly, taking in the little outdoor space. The patio was cozy, with a circular table and two chairs in the center, a flickering lantern casting a warm, golden glow over everything. Bougainvillea petals spilled over the walls, the pinks and purples glowing faintly in the light. He could see into Becca's apartment from here. She was curled up on the couch, legs tucked under her, reading a magazine. A glass of wine sat on the table in front of her.

She looked so peaceful. So... far from the chaos around them. It almost pained him to interrupt.

Moving forward, he let his presence be known, stepping

into the doorway. Her eyes snapped up, widening with fear. She opened her mouth, ready to scream, but he yanked off the balaclava and held a finger to his lips.

Her shoulders sagged in relief. "Shit," she breathed, pressing a hand to her chest. "You scared me."

"Sorry," he muttered, stepping inside. "This was the safest way in. I had to dodge the cameras."

She glanced toward the patio door, eyes still darting with lingering tension. Up close, he could see it—she wasn't as calm as she seemed. Her eyes were red-rimmed, and her face was pale. She'd been crying.

He frowned, lowering himself into the chair across from her. "What's going on?"

She bit her lip, her hands twisting in her lap. "Ramirez's wife," she said, voice low and shaky. "She was killed in a car crash this morning."

Ghost nodded, keeping his expression neutral. "I heard the men talking. I'm sorry. Did you know her well?"

Becca's hands clenched tighter. "We weren't that close, but..." She trailed off, struggling with her words. "I can't help thinking it wasn't an accident."

Ghost stiffened. His instincts flared immediately, a chill creeping down his spine. "You think someone caused the crash?"

She nodded, her lips trembling as she spoke. "Chrissy called me last night. She was upset—drinking, I think. She told me Ramirez was having an affair with the au pair and that she wanted to leave him. But he threatened her."

Ghost's jaw tightened. "Threatened her how?"

"She said if she left, she'd never see her daughters again."

"He was going to fight her for custody?"

Becca nodded. "Except, I called the airport. She'd booked three seats on a flight to Los Angeles this morning. She was on her way to get the girls when a truck barreled into her, killing her instantly."

Ghost was silent, letting her words sink in.

"Tell me that's a coincidence." Real fear flickered in her eyes.

"It does sound suspicious," he admitted. "Were there any witnesses?"

She shook her head. "No, only the truck driver, and he swears she ran a red light. It also happened in an industrial area with no cameras. If I were to pick a place to kill someone on that route, it would be there."

Ghost ran a hand through his hair. "Shit, Becca. Are you saying her husband had her killed?"

Becca sighed, frustration lining her face. "I don't know what I'm saying. I hope not, but…" She let the sentence trail off and took a sip of her wine. "Ramirez and Alek had an argument today. Alek called him a 'stupid bugger.' What do you think that means?"

Nothing good. And she was back to using first names.

Fuck. Why did this have to happen now, right before he had to leave? He wouldn't be around to protect her.

"Listen, Becca," he said, his tone urgent. "Ramirez is dangerous, and so is Markov. I agree—your friend's death sounds dodgy as hell. But don't go asking any more questions about it."

She blinked back tears. "I just want to know the truth."

"I know you do. But if what you're saying is true, Ramirez will go to great lengths to keep it buried."

She inhaled sharply, and Ghost knew his words had hit home. "You mean I could be in danger?"

"You already know too much. Promise me you won't dig any deeper."

"Okay, I promise."

He could see the fear etched into her face. "And don't tell anyone you spoke to Chrissy last night."

She gave a small nod, her hair falling forward, partially obscuring her face. Ghost moved closer, brushing the strands back gently. Her pupils were wide, dark, locked on his.

"I know he killed her, Dom. The bastard murdered his wife so he could live shack up with the nanny and keep his kids."

Ghost shook his head. That kind of thinking could get her killed. "I'm sorry for your loss, Becca, but you have to leave it alone. For now."

At her questioning look, he added, "I'm leaving. I'll be gone for a few days. That's what I came here to tell you."

Amongst other things.

"I didn't want to leave without saying goodbye."

Fear flashed in her eyes again. "Oh. When do you leave?"

"Tomorrow." He took her hand, her cool, clammy fingers fitting into his large, warm palm. "I wish I didn't have to go, but duty calls. The Colombians want their merchandise."

His words seemed to snap her out of her grief. She wiped at her eyes and sat straighter. "I'll be fine," she assured him. "You don't have to worry about me."

But he did. More than he should.

A pang shot through his chest as the realization hit. She was the one person in this godforsaken mess that he cared about. The thought of something happening to her…he couldn't even go there. But he didn't say any of that. He couldn't.

"I know. Just take care of yourself while I'm gone."

She sniffed. "You mean because I won't have you on speed dial?"

His gaze narrowed. "I mean it, Becca. These men are dangerous. I don't like the idea of leaving you here alone."

"I can take care of myself. I've been doing it for a long time."

He sighed. "I know you have, but these guys? They're different. They're killers, Becca. Ruthless. Your boss is wanted for attempted murder in the UK, Carlos was a guerrilla fighter for the FARC rebel group, and God only knows what Ramirez is capable of. And you're caught right in the middle. You really think Markov's just going to let you walk away one day? With everything you know? You might not think you're involved, but you are."

Her face paled, and Ghost immediately regretted his words. He didn't mean to scare her—or maybe he did. She needed to understand just how deep she was in.

Because he cared, dammit.

She was in way over her head. If only he could get her out of this cesspit, away from all the corruption. But he couldn't. Not yet. He needed her here. And he hated himself for it.

"You think they'd try to stop me from leaving?"

"One day, yes."

She swallowed hard. "I never thought of that before."

He had. He never gave anyone the benefit of the doubt, least of all scum-of-the-earth gun-runners like Markov and Ramirez. Occupational hazard, maybe, but it kept him alive.

"I'll help you." He lowered his voice. "I'll get you out. But right now, you need to promise me you'll keep your head down until I'm back."

Her lip quivered. "I promise."

He gazed into her deep brown eyes, and his heart twisted. She was so vulnerable, so scared. He wanted nothing more than to protect her, to keep her safe from the vipers circling. He reached out, and she moved into his arms like it was the most natural thing in the world.

"Hold me," she whispered.

CHAPTER 12

Becca wasn't usually the needy type, but tonight was different. Tonight, she craved the solidity of another human, someone strong enough to hold the chaos at bay, even if just for a moment. Between Chrissy's death and Dom's warning, she was unraveling.

What if he was right?

What if they figured out Chrissy had confided in her—or worse, that she suspected Ramirez had been behind his own wife's murder?

Dom closed the gap between them. His strong arms wrapped around her, crushing her against his chest. She buried her face in his neck, drawing in the warmth of him, the smell of him. His aftershave reminded her of the sea—and of safety. She tried to stifle the trembling sigh that escaped, but there was no use.

"It's alright," he murmured against her hair, his hand moving gently through it. "I've got you. I'm not going anywhere."

Her grip on him tightened. It didn't matter that Dom was

dangerous, that he'd been wrapped up in blood and violence long before she met him. Right now, he was her only anchor.

She looked up at him and his gaze scorched hers for a moment before his lips claimed hers, hard and insistent. She kissed him back, hoping to drive out the fear still gnawing at her insides.

Dom wasn't about gentle comfort. His intensity nearly knocked the air from her lungs, and when he kissed her again, it was with a fierce hunger. A reminder that he, too, was on the brink of losing control.

Becca gasped as he gripped her ass and lifted her up like she weighed nothing more than a child and settled her against him. Instinctively, she wrapped her legs around his waist.

Holy crap!

He was huge. There was no denying that. She could feel his impressive length, hard and aroused, pressing into her and the tension inside snapped. With a strangled sob, she clawed at him, desperate for more.

Tonight, she didn't want to feel like the woman hiding in the shadows, scared of the secrets she'd learned. She wanted to feel alive.

He held her tighter, his kiss growing more urgent, more chaotic. Her heart pounded, drowning out the doubts, the questions, the fear. There was nothing else but the two of them in that moment. The world outside could wait.

Dom's mouth moved against hers, rough and unrelenting, and Becca responded with a desperation she'd never felt before. She was done holding back, done feeling afraid. All the emotions she'd been burying for days surged forward, a wild need to feel something real, something that grounded her in the here and now.

Her hands fisted in his shirt, yanking him closer as if she could pull him inside her through sheer force of will. His heat, his strength—she wanted all of it, needed all of it. His body was like a furnace, pressing into hers, sending sparks down her spine, igniting something deep in her core. Her breath hitched as his hands moved to her hips, gripping her hard, holding her tight against him like he couldn't bear the space between them.

She gasped into his mouth, and heard Dom groan in response, the sound vibrating through her. Her skin was on fire, every nerve alive with need. She rolled her hips against him, feeling that hardness between her legs, and it was like a jolt of electricity straight to her core. Her body tightened, instinct taking over as she ground harder against him. The friction was maddening, almost enough to drive her over the edge right then.

"Dom..." she gasped, breaking the kiss to catch her breath.

Even the air felt charged, thick with the tension crackling between them. His hands slid under her dress, rough fingers brushing against her thighs, making her shudder. She was losing control, and she didn't care. She wanted him to take it from her, to be the one thing that made sense in a world that was spinning out of control.

He growled her name, his mouth trailing down her neck, teeth grazing her skin just enough to make her gasp. Her nails dug into his back, her body arching into him, desperate for more, for him.

His lips found the tender bruise on her collarbone, and the mix of pain and pleasure made her whimper. It wasn't enough. She needed him closer, deeper.

Her hands tangled in his hair, yanking his head back up to hers, claiming his mouth again with a hunger that matched his.

"Becca," he muttered against her lips, but she didn't let him finish. Her fingers slid down his chest, fumbling with the buttons of his shirt. She needed to feel him, his skin, his strength. Her hands shook as she ripped the last few buttons free, finally pushing the shirt off his shoulders.

The moment his bare chest pressed against hers, she let out a ragged moan. The feel of his skin against hers was like gasoline thrown on the fire raging inside her. She clung to him, her legs tightening around his waist, her hips rolling against him in frantic, needy movements.

Dom's breath was coming fast and shallow, his control slipping with every second, and it drove her wild.

She could feel it, the way he was fighting to hold back, but she didn't want him to. Not tonight. She wanted him raw, wanted him to let go as much as she needed to.

"Becca," he growled again, his voice rough and broken, but she didn't let him pull away.

"Please," she whispered, her voice hoarse and desperate as she moved against him, her entire body trembling with need. "Fuck me. Now."

CHAPTER 13

Fuck.

He couldn't hold on.

The desperation in Becca's voice said it all. Her hands gripped his shoulders, nails digging into his skin, pulling him closer like he was the only thing holding her together. She was breaking apart in front of him, and he had no choice but to catch her. His lips pressed hard against hers, feeding the hunger building between them.

Becca was wild, no longer thinking, just reacting. He helped her pull her panties down, before she pulled him deeper into the kiss, her body arching against him as though nothing could close the gap fast enough.

Somehow, in between kissing her, he managed to loosen his jeans and pull them down to his ankles, then he hoisted her onto the counter, her legs instantly wrapping around his waist. The rawness in her movements—so desperate, so fierce—pushed him to the edge.

His breath caught in his throat when she clawed at his chest, her fingers trembling but insistent. Her need was electric, making every nerve in his body fire like a live wire. He didn't bother fighting it. Hell, he'd wanted this just as much, maybe more.

He grabbed her hips and slammed her hard against him. Their bodies collided, and he sunk deep within her. No resistance, just a tight, hot sheath clenching around him.

She let out a gasping cry, and bit down on his lip. Christ, he'd never felt anything so intense, so magnificent.

Becca writhed against him, her hands everywhere—his chest, his back, pulling him closer, deeper, needing more. A frantic, primitive desire took over as he rushed headlong to meet her need. He gripped her hips, anchoring her on the counter as he drove repeatedly into her, hearing her gasps turn to moans and then to rasping cries.

"Oh, God. Dom!" Her head fell back, her chest rising and falling as she gasped his name. He loved hearing it. Loved knowing he was the cause of her delirium. She looked so beautiful with her full breasts bouncing erratically in front of him, her pink lips forming a little "O" and her dark hair cascading down her back.

Adrenaline and something he couldn't describe shot through him, and pounded into her, harder and harder, while gripping her hips and drawing her toward him for maximum penetration.

Shit, he was in so deep he could feel the end of her. With every thrust, her cries got louder, and soon he was grunting along with her, about to spiral over the edge.

"Becca..." he growled thickly trying to keep his focus but failing miserably. "Oh, shit, Becca. I don't know how much longer I can hang on."

Her only response was to pull him harder against her, grinding her hips with reckless abandon. Their movements became more frantic, more desperate. Her breath came in short, feverish bursts as she pressed her body against his, her hands clutching at him as though he was the only thing keeping her grounded.

Every kiss, every thrust was a fierce claim, an unspoken plea to drown out everything else—fear, grief, uncertainty.

Ghost's head spun, lost in the wild intensity of it all. He'd never seen her like this—so vulnerable, yet so powerful in her need. And God help him, he was right there with her.

He growled her name against her mouth, lost in the storm she'd pulled him into, knowing there was no way back.

Becca's legs stiffened around his waist. She was coming, he could feel it. He kept going, driving into her as hard and fast as he could. This was insane. Totally out of fucking control insane. His head was swimming. He was losing it.

Holy fuck!

She clenched around him, sending him flying over the abyss. Her fingers gripped his back, nails dragging along his skin as she cried out, convulsing around him over and over again. With every desperate thrust he exploded inside her, his vision blurring, and stars dancing at the edges. He kept going until he was completely and utterly drained.

Afterward, Becca leaned forward, dropping her damp forehead onto his chest. They were both slick with perspiration, their breaths labored gasps as they struggled to get themselves under control.

He held her, waiting for his head to clear, trying to formulate a sentence, but he was too shellshocked to speak. That had been the most intense, fucking out of this world crazy experience, a rush unlike nothing he'd ever experienced before.

He didn't know what it meant, but he knew it was something.

Something big.

And it scared the hell out of him.

CHAPTER 13

*B*ecca's head was swirling, spinning out of control, as if the world had just tilted on its axis.

Oh. My. God.

What the hell was that?

She could still feel his hands on her skin, the lingering heat of their bodies crashing together. And now? Now there was nothing but silence and the faint echo of her own heart pounding. It felt like she'd lost a piece of herself in that moment, something vital and wild, something she wasn't sure she could ever get back. What must he think of her now?

Embarrassed, she refused to meet his gaze. She couldn't. Her body screamed at her to look—look at him, at this man who had just wrecked her—but she didn't trust herself. The shame and confusion knotted in her chest too tightly. She needed space, needed air.

Without a word, she slid off the countertop, disentangling herself from his grip. Her body felt foreign, exposed, vulnerable. Her dress, once clinging to her skin, had fallen in the chaos, discarded like everything else. She could still feel the imprint of his hands all over her—rough, urgent, unapologetic. It was too much. She bent down, fumbling for the fabric, hastily buttoning it, though her hands trembled.

"You okay?" His voice was gentle, concerned.

Her throat tightened. She stole a glance at him and regretted it. He stood there, naked, glistening in the dim light like some kind of god. His chest, his abs, everything about him was carved from stone—perfect and infuriatingly calm.

Damn him. How could he look like that when she felt so broken?

"Yeah, I think so," she croaked, even though her throat felt like it was closing in on itself.

"Becca—"

"I don't want to talk about it, okay?" she cut him off, her voice sharper than she intended. She could feel her control slipping, unraveling at the edges. She didn't want to explain what had happened—she couldn't.

Dom's brow furrowed, surprise flickering in his eyes. But then he nodded, swallowing whatever he had been about to say. "Okay. If that's what you want."

It wasn't what she wanted. She didn't know what she wanted. But talking about it? Talking would make it real. How could she possibly explain what had just happened? How could she make him understand the storm raging inside her? That it wasn't just about him—it was everything. All the fear, the grief, the overwhelming sense that she was spiraling into something she couldn't control.

Her hands shook as she fumbled with the buttons of her dress, the silence stretching between them like a chasm she didn't know how to cross.

"It's a lot," she finally whispered, her voice brittle.

"I know," he said quietly.

Her gaze flicked up to meet his, and what she saw scared her even more than her own loss of control. Desire, confusion... tenderness. God, no. That wasn't part of the plan. It couldn't be.

Oh, boy.

"Do you want me to stay?" he asked.

She flinched at the question, her heart lurching. After everything that had just happened, how could she kick him out? But she needed to be alone. Needed to process what had happened, revel in the deliciousness of her reckless abandon, hold on to those moments and play them on repeat until she'd made some sense out of it.

Until then, she couldn't face him.

"No," she whispered. "I've got an early start."

He gave a simple nod, like he'd been expecting that answer. Was she that predictable? "That's okay," he said. "I have to pack anyway. Heading out around noon tomorrow."

He would have stayed if she'd wanted him to. Something tingled inside her, fluttering around her chest, but she shoved it down. There was no room for that right now.

"Where are you going?" It felt safer to talk about that. Something, anything, other than the whirlwind inside her.

"Back to Colombia." His tone darkened, and he didn't need to say more. She knew what it meant—another shipment, more danger. He was stepping back into the fire, where men like him lived.

"You'll be careful, won't you?" The words slipped out before she could stop them. Shit. That sounded too much like she cared, like she couldn't bear the thought of him getting hurt.

His lips quirked. "I always am."

She nodded, turning away to hide her flaming cheeks.

"Becca?"

She froze. "Yeah."

"There's something I need to tell you."

Her stomach dropped, and her heart clenched. Oh, no.

Here it comes. The part where he tells her it was a mistake. Or that he's married. Or has a girlfriend. She braced herself for the excuses, the same ones she'd heard a dozen times before, already shrinking away from the blow.

"What?"

"Turn around."

Reluctantly, she did, watching as he bent to pull up his jeans, fastening the zipper with deliberate slowness. She breathed a silent sigh of relief. Thank goodness. It was too hard to look at him naked. Too raw. Her mind kept replaying what had just happened, her body still buzzing from the way he had touched her, held her, the way he had wrecked her. "What did you want to tell me?"

Dom hesitated, his gaze searching hers for something. He opened his mouth, then closed it, his jaw ticking like he was trying to figure out the right words. Finally, he spoke. "I'm not who you think I am."

Her stomach twisted. Oh, God. Here we go.

"You're married, aren't you? I knew it. There had to be something." She threw it out there, hoping to get it over with, to cut through the tension.

"No," he shook his head, a bitter smile tugging at his lips. "You're safe on that front. But it's my job I lied about."

"What?" Becca stared at him, the words not quite sinking in. His job? "You can't get much worse than a drug-smuggling mercenary."

Dom snorted, but there was no humor in it. "That depends on how you look at it."

"Dom, you're worrying me. What is it?"

He exhaled sharply, his jaw popping again. Whatever he was about to say, it was hard for him to get out. She could see that.

"I'm still in the Marine Corps," he finally said, his voice low, almost ashamed. "I never left. I'm undercover."

She blinked, the weight of his words taking a moment to register. Undercover... still in the Marines?

"You didn't go AWOL?" she whispered.

He shook his head. "I was recruited by someone in Suarez's organization. They were poaching soldiers to use as mercs, so I went undercover to find out what was going on. Once I was inside, the DEA got wind of it and asked me to feed them intel on his drug trafficking network."

"Alberto Suarez?" She swallowed, a lump forming in her throat. He was as infamous as Pablo Escobar in these parts.

"The one and only," Dom admitted.

"Didn't he get caught? I remember reading about it a couple of months ago." Then it clicked, and her eyes widened. "Wait a minute, was that you?"

"Indirectly. My intel is what got him busted. He walked right into a DEA sting operation."

Becca gripped the counter as the pieces fell into place. "And now you're undercover in Alek Markov's organization?"

Dom nodded.

"Oh, shit."

She ran a hand through her hair. All this time, she'd thought he was a violent gun for hire, a mercenary working for her boss, when really, he was... a good guy.

Somehow, the bad guy had been easier to accept.

"Are you going to bust him too? For smuggling guns to Colombia?"

Dom's chest rose as he exhaled. "I'm going to try. But right now, we don't have much. Markov doesn't put his name on anything official. He uses dummy corporations for all his illegal transactions. On paper, he's squeaky clean." He studied her, his gaze intense. "That's why I need your help."

Her stomach dropped. "My help?"

"Yeah. I know it's a lot to ask, but if you can get into his study and look for evidence of the arms deal with the

Colombians, we might have something. Documents, emails, anything that ties him to the deal."

Becca shook her head before he even finished. "I handle his legitimate business. I don't have access to any of that stuff. And Alek wouldn't be stupid enough to leave incriminating evidence lying around in his office or on his laptop."

"You're probably right, but I'm out of options, Becca. The deal's happening in a few days, and I've got nothing. If Markov isn't at the handover himself—and he won't be—there's no proof he was involved."

"What about Ramirez?" she asked, her mind jumping to the one man she would gladly see locked away forever. She was convinced he'd had his wife killed.

"Ramirez's name is all over this. We can arrest him and put him away for a hundred years based on what we already have, but he's small fry compared to Markov."

Becca turned and stepped out onto the patio. The night was still and warm, but it did nothing to soothe her growing unease. In the distance, the waves crashed rhythmically against the shore. "I'm sorry, Dom. I wish I could help you, but I can't."

She heard him follow her outside. His arms wrapped around her from behind, pulling her into his chest. "I'm sorry. Forget I asked. It's too dangerous." He kissed the back of her neck, his lips soft against her skin. "I just spent the night warning you not to investigate your friend's death, and here I am asking you to spy on your boss."

She could feel his heart beating steadily against her back.

"It's not that," she said quietly.

Dom's arms tightened slightly, but she stepped out of his embrace. This time, she couldn't let him hold her together.

"What is it, then?"

Becca turned to face him, her voice barely a whisper. "I can't help you dig up dirt on Alek—because he's my father."

CHAPTER 14

"What the—?"

Ghost staggered backward, trying to process what she'd just said.

"Alek Markov is your father?"

Becca nodded, her expression pained, misery etched into every line of her face. "I'd love to help you, I really would, but how can I betray my own father?"

Ghost's brain stuttered. It wasn't often he was left speechless, but standing there, staring at her, his thoughts collided like a freight train.

"I'm sorry," she whispered into the thick silence. "I should've told you before, but no one knows. Not even Ramirez. I hadn't seen Alek for ten years. Not until he showed up at the embassy and... convinced me to work for him. It was an olive branch, you know? A way to reconnect after being estranged. I thought maybe... maybe he deserved a second chance."

He exhaled hard, the air rushing from his lungs like he'd been punched. It all started to make sense now—the way Markov watched her, how she deferred to him, called him

Alek instead of the cold detachment she had with everyone else. She was his blood.

And he hadn't seen it.

Fuck.

He'd compromised himself. Two years of undercover work, blown to pieces in a single night because he couldn't keep it in his pants.

Because of *her*.

The heat between them, that wild, mind-shattering sex...

But this was more than lust, more than the mission. She'd burrowed under his skin, made him reckless.

Pat would kill him. He'd blown his cover for what? A moment of connection? Of need? What the hell was he thinking?

He started pacing the patio, frustration churning inside him. His mind raced with a dozen thoughts, each more damning than the last. How could he fix this? How could he possibly salvage what he'd just destroyed?

Becca watched him warily, like a deer staring down a lion that had just tasted blood. "I won't tell," she whispered, her voice thin and trembling. Fear flickered in her eyes, a spark of uncertainty that gutted him.

Damn it. He hated himself for putting it there.

"It's not that," he lied, his voice gruff. "I just can't believe I didn't see it sooner." Some undercover agent he was.

"How could you have?" She sank into one of the patio chairs, shoulders slumped. "Alek didn't want anyone to know. He said his enemies would use me to get to him."

Ghost clenched his fists. She was right. Markov had plenty of enemies, and she'd be the perfect pawn. A prime target.

"I never would've asked you to help me if I'd known," Dom muttered, guilt washing over him.

She glanced up, her eyes filled with questions he couldn't

answer. "And you wouldn't have told me who you really were, either. Would you?"

He didn't respond. They both knew the truth.

"And just now?" Her voice wavered, barely holding steady. "Was that all a part of it? Did you come here to seduce me into helping you spy on him?"

"Of course not." He tried to meet her gaze but couldn't. It was more complicated than that. He didn't know how to explain it, how to separate his feelings from the mission.

She dropped her head, a bitter laugh escaping her lips. "I see."

"Becca, it's not like that. What just happened, it was real. It meant something."

"Please, Dom, don't make this worse. I'd like to keep what's left of my dignity."

His throat tightened. What could he say? He had come here to ask her to help him, but he hadn't expected the flood of emotions, the connection that had sparked between them. It had all gotten tangled up in a way he hadn't seen coming.

"I'd like you to leave now."

"Becca, please. We can talk this through."

"There's nothing else to say."

He hesitated, his feet rooted to the spot, unwilling to move.

Her face hardened, her voice sharp. "What did you expect, Dom? A happily ever after?"

"What? You don't believe in happily ever after?"

Neither did he, but that was beside the point.

"No such thing. It was just sex." She turned away from him and walked inside, her voice softening in resignation. "You know the way out."

And just like that, she dismissed him.

He stood there like an idiot, staring after her.

Well done, Dom. Way to screw everything up.

Eventually, he followed her inside, bending to grab his shirt from the lounge floor. He pulled it on, the scent of her still clinging to the fabric like a cruel reminder of what they'd just shared.

She was in the kitchen, her back stiff, her hands gripping the counter. Her whole body was rigid, vibrating with tension.

"He's a bad man, Becca," he said softly. "There are things he's done that shouldn't go unpunished."

"I know." Her voice broke on a whisper. "But he's still my dad. And I've only just gotten him back."

Dom clenched his jaw, frustration biting at him. "He doesn't deserve your loyalty. If things go south, he'll throw you to the wolves without a second thought."

"You don't know that," she shot back, turning to face him, her eyes blazing with anger and fear.

"I do. He's a psychopath, Becca. He cares about one thing —himself."

For a moment, her expression faltered. He could see the doubt, the fear of what she already knew but wouldn't admit.

"If you want to take him down, fine," she spat. "But don't use me to do it."

"I won't." His voice was rough with emotion. "I just hope you don't get caught in the crossfire. This deal is happening, whether you like it or not. The authorities are out for blood. We couldn't arrest him in the U.S., but he's going down for this, one way or another."

Her shoulders slumped, the fight draining out of her. "He's all I've got, Dom."

He didn't correct her, but she was wrong. She had him too, she just didn't know it yet.

CHAPTER 15

Ghost crouched beneath the dense jungle canopy, ten clicks from the Colombian border. The air hung heavy with humidity, and the ancient roots of the kapok tree snaked around him like veins through the earth, pressing up against his boots. He could feel their weight underfoot.

Dammit, Becca.

He hated how they'd left things. She thought he'd used her, seduced her to get to Markov.

And the worst part? She wasn't wrong.

But it hadn't just been about sex. That was what really twisted him up inside—it had meant something, something real. How the hell could he make her see that, especially after what she'd told him?

For fuck's sake.

Markov's daughter. Pat sure as hell hadn't seen that coming. Blackthorn Security had dug into her past but had turned up nothing beyond her being born to an unmarried mother in North Carolina. No father listed on her birth certificate, no hints of a connection to Markov. Typical. The bastard didn't put his name on anything.

Rebecca Lyndall.

She'd lived with her father for a couple years in California after her mother passed away. But no one had linked her to Alek Markov. Hell, he'd checked her out himself before he left the hacienda—cross-referenced her DMV records and seen her old photo. Even back then, she was stunning.

His gut twisted at the thought of eighteen-year-old Becca trying to reconnect with Markov, only to discover the man's cold indifference. No wonder they'd been estranged. What a colossal disappointment that must have been for her.

A drop of rain slapped his head, followed by a steady drizzle. The rhythmic pitter-patter of rain on the jungle's broad leaves usually calmed him. Not today.

It didn't matter, he needed to stay alert. The border wasn't far away, but in dense forest such as this, it may as well have been a hundred miles. The Darien Gap, the most dangerous stretch of jungle on the planet was rife with criminales, guerilla fighters, displaced rebels and all manner of scumbags. If he let his guard down, he'd be finished. It only took one bullet, and his body would lie here until it rotted. No one would ever find him.

Where the hell was the fisherman?

As if on cue, he heard the low chug of a motor coming down the river. Ghost checked his rifle, scanning the surroundings with practiced eyes. The Darien Gap's twisting waterways were perfect for smuggling everything from guns to drugs—and sometimes people.

He crouched lower, his boots sinking into the mud as the dark, narrow motorboat rounded the bend. The soft splutter of its engine barely cut through the thick, humid air. Perfect camouflage. It took someone with trained eyes to spot it at all.

Biri, the wiry fisherman, steered the boat toward the bank. His weathered face, hunched back, and wiry frame told a story of years working these waters. He used to be a simple fisherman, living off the land. Now, thanks to men like Suarez—and more recently Markov—he was ferrying drugs and weapons.

Ghost had become his best client, securing his loyalty with cold, hard cash. That money had rebuilt Biri's house, sent his son to school.

Who said a life of crime didn't pay?

Ghost didn't kid himself—Biri would keep working for whoever paid, long after Markov was in prison.

It was the job of the Panamanian border enforcement authorities to keep the drugs out and guard the border, but it was a difficult, if not impossible task. The routes were varied and changeable, the load was disseminated and erratic, and mules and distributors were armed and dangerous, and often knew the slopes of the impenetrable Gap better than the crews patrolling them.

On the Colombian side, the military did border checks, but only in the navigable sections, which were few and far between.

The official border post was just a small clearing in the jungle, but all around it were endless hills, muddy rivers and swampland choked with vegetation. And that wasn't counting the thorns, wasps, snakes and wild animals.

"Hell on earth," his former commander at the training center had described it. He wasn't wrong.

All this just worked in Ghost's favor and made it harder for the authorities to catch him. He had the skillset, compliments of the Marine Corps, and he'd honed his craft working for Suarez. He gave a snort and swung his rifle over his shoulder. Now Markov was reaping the benefits.

The truck driver who'd dropped off the crates was long gone. No one stuck around these parts longer than they had to. But now it was time to move.

Ghost waded into the murky water, helping Biri drag the boat onto the mossy bank. He handed him a bottle of water, and Biri gulped it down, nodding his thanks.

Together, they started loading the crates. Twenty in total. Heavy and awkward, each one filled with weapons bound for Colombia. Sweat trickled down Ghost's neck as they heaved the last crate into the boat.

Biri might have a crooked spine, but the man was as strong as an ox. Ghost had seen plenty of hard men in his time, but Biri—this man had survived the jungle. The two shook hands, and just as Biri climbed into the boat, Ghost heard it—the unmistakable roar of high-powered engines, growing louder by the second.

Fuck.

Panamanian border patrol. The sound was unmistakable. This deep in the jungle, it was either them or the Colombian military, and neither option was good.

"Vamanos," Ghost growled, already back in the boat.

The fisherman was quicker than Ghost expected, pushing off the bank and revving the engine. Ghost wasted no time in leaping in with him, backpack and all. He wasn't going to wait around for armed militia to spray him down, or worse, arrest him and shove him in a stinking Panamanian jail.

They shot off downriver into the swampland and towards the Colombian border. The drone of the pursuing motorboats got louder, but the myriads of twists in the river meant they were still invisible.

Biri, gripping the wheel like his life depended on it, spotted a tiny, overgrown inlet. He cut the engine, letting the boat glide into the thick brush. They ducked, branches and vines slapping their faces as they pushed deeper into the jungle's green labyrinth.

Ghost's heart hammered in his chest as the boat drifted to a stop. The loud, mechanical growl of the patrol boats filled the air. They'd been spotted. He was sure of it.

"Son of a bitch," he muttered under his breath. Biri didn't need to be told—they both knew what was coming.

The engines cut out, and the jungle fell eerily silent.

Ghost crouched low, rifle in hand, ready to bail and dive into the river if they got too close. He was an expert at escape and evasion, but there was no way to know if they'd been tracked. If their pursuers opened fire, they'd be dead in minutes.

Biri's eyes were wide with fear, his hand hovering over the shotgun stashed beneath the seat. But Ghost knew better than to go loud.

There were too many of them.

This was an organized bust—they'd be outgunned and outflanked in seconds. Sweat poured off him as he focused on the water's edge, watching for any sign of movement. The silence was suffocating.

A rustle. Then, the menacing steel nose of a patrol boat poked through the foliage.

CHAPTER 16

*I*t was game over.

Ghost edged to the side of the boat, ready to slip into the water when a sharp shout cut through the air.

Biri shot up a hand. *Wait.*

Ghost froze, heart hammering.

"Por aquí!" a voice called in Spanish. "This way!"

There was a grunt, followed by the low mechanical growl of the patrol boat's engine shifting into reverse.

Ghost held his breath. *Thank fuck.*

Unbelievable. The patrol boat backed out of the inlet, disappearing into the muddy tributary. Within moments, the deep hum of three boats roared off down the river. They must've decided the smugglers had made a break for the Colombian border. The Panamanians wouldn't cross over. Even if they did, that part of the river was a mess of swamp and tangled vegetation. Good luck finding anything in there.

Biri exhaled loud and long, and Ghost let out a shaky chuckle. They grinned at each other like idiots before collapsing onto the deck, adrenaline crashing hard.

"Let's sit tight till we're in the clear," Ghost muttered. The patrol boats wouldn't get far before turning around. The river ahead was more marsh than water, and they'd have to double back. "We need to camouflage the boat, just in case."

Biri nodded, already grabbing handfuls of reeds and muck. They worked in silence, covering the boat with slimy vegetation until it blended into the jungle around them. From the river, it would just look like another gnarled trunk swallowed by the undergrowth.

Then they waited.

Biri dozed off, while Ghost kept watch. Not much was happening. A troop of monkeys swung by, chittering at the strange humans below. Ghost swatted at a relentless cloud of tapa flies, but otherwise, the jungle was quiet.

An hour crawled by before they heard the boats again, the patrols heading back to base. This time, the noise faded fast, engines cutting into the distance.

They were clear.

Biri stirred and stretched, rolling to his feet. "I go now."

Ghost gave a short nod. Colombia wasn't somewhere he wanted to end up today. Biri knew what to do—he'd handled the handoff plenty of times before.

The two men shook hands, and Ghost stepped out of the boat into the thick, wet brush. Water seeped into his boots immediately, soaking the bottom of his pants. He pushed the boat into the current, gave Biri a brief wave, then turned and slogged his way toward the shore.

Ghost looked around, getting his bearings. He was in deep—way farther south than he'd planned. Pulling out his compass, he tried to figure out the quickest way back. If he could hit the logging trail, it'd save him days of hiking, but to get there, he'd have to cross miles of impenetrable jungle and a fast-flowing river. Still better than the alternative.

He set off, ducking under low-hanging branches, climbing over aerial roots, and squelching through mud.

Once he hit the logging station, he could hitch a ride back into town. For now, he just had to keep moving.

With the adrenaline fading, his thoughts drifted back to the ambush. That hadn't been an accident.

As he trudged through the muck, Ghost mentally checked off the people who could've leaked their route to the authorities. Much as he hated himself for it, the first name that popped into his head was Becca.

Had she ratted him out?

No. He dismissed the thought as quickly as it came. If Becca had turned him in, she'd be betraying her father too. Besides, she didn't know their exact route, and the border patrol had known exactly where to look. No, Becca wasn't the type.

He scowled and hacked through a tangle of vines with his machete. Rain started to trickle through the canopy, but the dense leaves above shielded him from the worst of it. This rainforest had one of the highest annual rainfalls in the world, and the swampy delta he'd just left was proof. The entire region was like a web of interconnected puddles, all fed by the rivers snaking down from the purple hills of the Darien Reserve.

Next up on his list: Markov's crew.

Ramirez loved his position, the money and power that came with it. He wasn't going to blow up his own operation by tipping off the authorities. No motive.

Carlos? He didn't know the details of the op. Sure, he had access to the cameras and mics in the hacienda, but Ghost only discussed plans in Markov's office. The place was swept for bugs at least once a day. Markov wasn't stupid. He was paranoid as hell.

Up ahead, a narrow river sliced through the jungle, fast and swollen from the rain. The ground was slick, the steep incline making it tricky to navigate. Ghost shrugged off his pack, stuffed it into a plastic liner, and tied it to his leg with rope. Wading into the river, the icy water hit him like a punch to the gut.

Damn, that was freezing.

He forced his breathing to stay even and crossed as quickly as he could, eyes scanning for anything lurking beneath the surface that might want to take a chunk out of him. In a place like this, one mistake could cost him more than just time.

Once on the other side, soaked but alive, he continued downstream. If he kept his bearings right, he'd hit the logger's drop-off point in a couple of hours.

His mind shifted to his own crew. He didn't want to think it, but someone had to be the rat. How else did the patrol know where to ambush them?

He started at the top: Jesús and Pedro. They'd been in the game too long to snitch, unless someone had gotten to them. They had families, and when push came to shove, you could make anyone talk if you pressed the right buttons. Still, they didn't know enough to sell out the whole operation.

Jonny, the logger, was solid. An ex-pat with a criminal record back in the States, he'd burned that bridge a long time ago. Panama was his safe haven. If he sold them out, he'd be cutting his own throat.

Biri had been just as shocked by the ambush as Ghost, so it wasn't him. And Miguel? He was on the Colombian side of the border. If he'd flipped, the attack would've come from the south.

Shit. Back to square one.

The rain started to pick up again, heavy drops splattering against the leaves overhead. The sky was darkening. Soon, it'd be too dangerous to travel. Navigating this jungle in daylight was tough enough. At night? Impossible.

Ghost scouted for a place to hunker down. Sleeping out

here wasn't fun, but he had the gear to string up a hammock between two trees and ration packs to get him through. He could live off the land if he had to—there were decent fish in the rivers—but he wasn't in the mood for that tonight.

As he settled in, his thoughts drifted, unbidden, back to Becca. What was she doing right now?

Hard to believe that this time last night, he'd been inside her. Hell, he wanted to call it making love, but they both knew that wasn't what it was. It had been raw. Urgent. Desperate. He could still smell her hair, taste her skin.

Fuck.

Why had he gone and told her who he was? It had wrecked whatever this thing between them was. He didn't think she'd run to her father, but if it came down to it, whose side would she take?

He exhaled, long and slow.

He exhaled noisily. He thought he knew—and it wasn't his.

CHAPTER 17

Becca lay in bed, staring at the ceiling, thinking about the man who had brought her to the brink of something raw and intense just twenty-four hours ago.

Where was he now?

Probably deep in the jungle, hauling her father's illegal merchandise through rebel-infested terrain, surrounded by criminals, danger lurking in every shadow.

She missed him. His scent, the roughness of his touch, the heat of his body pressed against hers. Hell, she missed everything about him.

Her heart sank. She'd fallen for him—it hit her like a punch to the gut. Hard. Unavoidable. Even though he was supposed to be the enemy.

Or was he?

It had been easier when she thought he was just a badass mercenary, wrapped up in the same muddy waters she was. At least then, they'd been on the same side. The rules were simple—survival, profit, no questions asked.

Now everything was upside down. Dom wasn't just another hired gun. He was the guy gunning for her father.

The good guy, doing what he thought was right, setting up her old man just like he'd set up Suarez.

But she couldn't hate him for it. He wasn't wrong. Not about her father, at least.

So where did that leave her?

She turned over, punching her pillow in frustration, trying to force herself into some semblance of comfort. Her father was one of the most dangerous men in Central America—everyone knew that. And by staying silent, she was complicit. She wasn't running the guns, or laundering the money, but wasn't turning a blind eye just as bad?

God, what was she doing?

The heat in her room became unbearable. She kicked the sheets off and stumbled to the window, pushing it open. Outside, the rain was soft, pattering against the dense jungle, a muted sound that echoed the turmoil inside her. It wasn't like rain on city streets—no harsh splatter on concrete, no cars splashing through puddles. It was gentler, more natural, almost soothing. Except she couldn't relax.

She leaned out, inhaling deeply. The air smelled different out here too—clean, like freshly cut grass and damp earth. She wondered if it was raining where Dom was. Was he huddled under a shelter, waiting it out? Or did he not even care? Rain was probably just another thing to endure for a man like him.

Was he thinking of her?

Shaking her head, she climbed back into bed, pulling the covers up to her chin. Closing her eyes, she remembered how alive she'd felt in his arms. She tried to recapture the feeling of safety, of rightness, from that night. For a few precious moments, she could almost believe it. Almost forget about the lies and the looming storm of betrayal.

But it didn't last. Soon she was tossing and turning again, her thoughts swirling with questions she had no answers to.

The sun was poking its head over the horizon when her body finally succumbed to sleep.

Later that morning, Becca sat at her desk, bleary-eyed and unfocused, entering the receipts from housekeeping into the accounting software. It was a routine she did monthly, more out of habit than necessity. There wasn't really a budget to stick to, but it gave her something to show Alek at the end of the month. More importantly, it kept her mind from spiraling into the chaos she couldn't control.

She froze at the sound of tires crunching over gravel, her heart skipping a beat. She'd done this a dozen times today—rushed to the window at every car that pulled up, hoping. But this time, she got lucky.

It was *him*.

Her pulse quickened as she watched Dom climb out of a khaki Jeep, dirty from the road but somehow more imposing for it. The vehicle was perfect for rough terrain, but what surprised her most was that he was driving—alone.

Before she could process that, Carlos stormed into the quad, flanked by two burly guards, weapons drawn. Rapid-fire Spanish erupted between them, Carlos gesturing wildly as if Dom's very presence here unaccompanied was an affront.

"What the fuck is he doing here by himself?" Alek's voice boomed as he stormed out of his study, the door flying open with a bang.

Becca straightened, trying to hide the smile tugging at her lips. "He was special forces, don't forget. He probably knew the location of the hacienda this whole time."

Alek glowered, pacing to the window. "He's showing off," he muttered. "Coming here unannounced just to prove he can. The bastard's trying to make a point."

Becca's eyes followed Dom as he stalked toward the main house. His face was set in a grim line, dirt smeared across his jaw, his eyes burning with something darker. "I don't think it's just that. He looks... pissed."

Her father squinted, but Dom was already out of sight, Carlos still gesturing uselessly after him.

"We're about to find out," Alek muttered, irritation lining his features as he crossed his arms, waiting.

Becca's heart did a flip as Dom strode into the office. Despite his filthy, disheveled state—he smelled like mud, his clothes soaked through—it was good to see him. She had to bite her tongue not to ask if he was okay.

Alek beat her to it. "What the hell happened to you? You look like you just crawled out of the damn jungle."

"I did." Dom's voice was a low growl, cutting to the point as he jerked his head toward Alek's study. "We need to talk. Now."

Becca stepped aside, feeling a strange pang of disappointment as Dom brushed past her without even a glance. He didn't so much as acknowledge her. The distance stung more than she cared to admit. It was as if whatever they'd shared didn't matter now that they were on opposite sides.

But they weren't really on opposite sides, were they? He wanted Alek locked up, and she... she wasn't exactly opposing him. She just wasn't helping. It felt like sitting on a fence, watching a war play out, unsure which way to fall.

Still, the way he'd ignored like a stranger stung. As if what had happened between them the other night was nothing.

She sighed, dropping heavily into her desk chair. The numbers on the screen blurred, and after a few minutes of staring, she gave up entirely and drifted toward Alek's office. The door was thick, soundproofed, but she caught fragments of the conversation—"ambush" and "patrols."

Her heart sank. That didn't sound good.

Had the shipment been compromised? Ambushed by border patrol? And if so, how had Dom made it out? The questions bubbled up inside her, but she knew the answers weren't coming anytime soon.

"What's going on?" Ramirez's sudden voice behind her made her jump. He appeared in the doorway, his gaze sharp. "I heard Dominguez arrived without escort. Carlos is furious. Why are you standing outside the door?"

"I was about to ask if they wanted tea," she muttered, trying to sound casual, though the sharpness of Ramirez's stare unnerved her. There was something calculating in his expression, something that reminded her too much of the way he might have looked when giving the order to have his wife killed.

She knocked on the door, her heart thumping.

"What?" Alek's irritated voice rang out.

"Ramirez is here. Should I send him in?"

Alek nodded curtly.

She opened the door, letting Ramirez pass, then hesitated. "Do you need anything?" she asked, already knowing the answer.

Alek shook his head. "No."

Becca closed the door and backed away. Maybe it was better not to know what was being discussed in there. After all, she was only here to reconnect with her father, not to get involved in his criminal operations. At least, that's what she kept telling herself.

Restless, she headed down to the kitchen to make herself a coffee. She wasn't about to hang around the office like a lovesick puppy waiting for a glimpse of Dom. She had some dignity left.

Outside, the kitchen door was propped open. Fernando, the chef, stood in the doorway, cigarette in hand. He glanced at her as she stepped out. "I heard shouting when Señor Dominguez arrived," he said, his voice low. "Carlos is very, very angry." He chuckled, blowing out a long stream of smoke.

Becca forced a smile. There weren't many men who could piss off Carlos and get away with it, but Dom was one of them. That didn't mean Carlos wouldn't make him pay for it later. Men like that held grudges. Dom would have to watch his back.

"Is there trouble coming, Miss Becca?" Fernando's voice was suddenly serious, the lightness gone. His dark eyes held a weight that made her stomach clench.

"Why would you ask that?" she turned to face him, surprised by the anxiety in his expression.

He shrugged, flicking the ash off his cigarette. "Just got a bad feeling. You tell us if trouble's coming, okay?"

She swallowed hard. By *us*, he meant the staff—the gardener, the maid, Fernando himself. The ones who had nothing to do with the darker side of her father's business. The innocent ones. Somehow, she felt comforted by being lumped in with them. It reminded her she had a choice.

"I will," she promised, hoping she could keep her word.

"Becca, can we talk?"

Crap.

Becca jerked at the sound of Dom's voice, spilling coffee onto her wrist. Fernando's eyebrows lifted, but he quietly stubbed out his cigarette and headed inside, shooting her a curious look as he went.

Dom was taking a risk, talking to her out here where anyone could see them, where Fernando had seen them.

She stood, her pulse quickening. "What are you doing out here? You shouldn't be seen talking to me."

"I need to talk to you." His voice was low but urgent.

She glanced around before nodding, leading him further

to the side of the house where the trash bins were stacked. If someone came by, at least they'd be out of view.

"What is it? What happened? Are you okay?" Her eyes roamed over him—disheveled, covered in grime, and clearly exhausted. Up close, he smelled like the jungle itself.

"Becca, we were ambushed. Someone leaked the smuggling route to the Panamanian authorities. There was a patrol waiting for us near the Colombian border."

Her eyes widened. "Oh my God. Are you okay?" She scanned him for injuries, but he seemed intact.

"I'm fine. But it was close."

"Who do you think it was?" She braced herself for his answer, dread building in her chest.

His silence spoke volumes. His eyes flicked to hers.

"It wasn't me!" she snapped, a flare of anger mixing with her fear. "How dare you think I'd betray my own father!"

His jaw clenched. "I didn't say you did. But I had to ask."

She crossed her arms, glaring. "Why would I do that? I don't even know the details of your damn arms smuggling operation."

Dom sighed, rubbing a hand across his face. "I didn't think it was you. I just wanted to hear you say it."

Her anger faded, replaced by a knot of anxiety. "What are you going to do now?"

"I need to figure out who tipped them off. Sabotaging the route is one thing, but risking lives? That's a whole different level of betrayal."

She scoffed, her heart racing. "You think we're enemies now, don't you?"

"I don't know what we are." His voice was hard, but there was something beneath it—something raw.

Becca bit her lip, feeling the weight of his words. They were on a collision course, the both of them. And yet, standing here, she couldn't hate him. Not when all she wanted to do was reach out and hold him.

"I'm not against you, Dom," she whispered. "But I won't betray my father, either."

He stared at her for a moment, eyes unreadable. "You're already involved, whether you like it or not."

Her breath caught. This was getting dangerous, fast.

"I'm scared," she admitted softly, more to herself than him.

"You should be." His voice was grim. "And that's why I'm telling you—get out. Leave this place while you still can."

Her heart twisted at his words. "I ran away once before. I can't do it again."

Dom's gaze softened. "This isn't running away, Becca. This is survival. And trust me, a Panamanian jail is no place for someone like you."

Tears pricked at her eyes. "I can't just leave. There's more to my father than you know."

Dom's brow furrowed, his eyes narrowing. "What do you mean?"

Becca swallowed hard, the weight of her secret pressing down on her. "There are things about Alek... things you should know before you do anything."

CHAPTER 18

*B*ecca walked onto the wooden deck and gazed out at the sun hovering over the horizon, still blazing, but without its usual intensity. After work, she'd turned down her father's offer for dinner, saying there was something she needed to take care of, and slipped away to see Dom at his beachfront cabin. They needed to talk.

This time the coast was clear, and she didn't run into Carlos or anyone else.

"What did you want to tell me?" Dom asked, coming to stand beside her.

There were two loungers on the deck, but this wasn't a casual chat. Becca felt better standing, while delivering this news.

She took a nervous breath. "I wanted to tell you about the first time I met my father."

He gave a curious nod, probably wondering why she was telling him this now.

She'd never told anyone this, but suddenly, she needed to get it out. Needed him to understand. "After my mother passed, I went to San Francisco to look for Alek. All I had to go on was a name my mother had written in her diary. To my surprise, he was easy to find. A successful businessman, he lived in this sprawling mansion in the hills, with servants, a tennis court, even a lake. It was like something out of a movie."

She paused, collecting her thoughts. Dom didn't interrupt.

"At first, things were awkward between us, but as time went by, he warmed to me—or so I thought. Eventually, he asked me to move into his mansion. I was running out of money, so I agreed. I thought it would bring us closer together. It was while I was there that I met Damian."

Dom's eyes narrowed. "Who's Damian?"

She hesitated. "He was this young, hot-shot computer programmer who worked for my father. Apparently—and I didn't know this at the time—my father conducted a lot of business on the dark web. Damian was his cyber guru. Together they sold millions of dollars of merchandise on the black market using a form of cryptocurrency that Damian invented."

"Like bitcoin?" asked Dom.

She nodded. "Just like that, although with Damian's currency, it was easier to remain anonymous."

Dom nodded.

"Anyway, we began dating. He also lived at the mansion, along with several other full-time employees. Alek's business empire was vast and extended across many different sectors."

Dom had gone very still.

"Alek funded Damian's cryptocurrency startup. He invested large amounts of money into it, mainly because it was benefitting him directly, and it was a legitimate front for his less respectable undertakings."

"Was he dealing arms at that point?" Dom asked.

Becca shrugged. "I think so. He was born in the Czech

Republic and had a lot of contacts there. He used to fly to Eastern Europe all the time on 'business trips.' In the beginning, I had no idea what he was involved in—I was just happy to have found him—but as the months went by and I got closer to Damian, I realized what he was really up to."

"And Damian was happy to be Alek's facilitator?" he asked scornfully.

She sighed. "It was complicated. Damian was a good guy deep down, but he'd gotten into a bad crowd at a young age. I know that doesn't excuse it, but he made the best out of a bad situation. He was a computer hacker before Alek took him under his wing."

"You sure like the bad boys, don't you?" Dom murmured.

She flushed. "Like I said, he wasn't a bad guy. In fact, it was shortly after that when Damian began acting strangely. The business was going well, but his relationship with my father was under strain. I didn't know what was going on, I just knew they weren't getting along like they used to. Then one day, he said he wanted out."

"Can't blame him," said Dom.

Becca continued as if he hadn't spoken. Reliving the moment her life had fallen apart wasn't easy. "Alek came up with this crazy idea that if we got married, Damian would be tied to him forever. He'd threatened to leave, he was even prepared to sacrifice the company, but he knew too much about my father's black-market dealings. Alek couldn't let him leave. I was afraid for him." She paused, gnawing on her lip. "So, we got engaged."

Dom gawked at her.

"I didn't want to do it," she said quickly, "but I was scared. I didn't want anything to happen to Damian. By that stage, I knew Alek well enough to know that people who crossed him had a way of disappearing. So, I planted the idea in Damian's head, and a few weeks later, he proposed."

Dom shook his head.

"I always felt bad about that. You see," Becca's voice broke, "Damian loved me."

Dom studied her, an inscrutable expression on his face. "You didn't love him back?"

"I think I did love him a little, but I wasn't madly in love, no." She sighed. "As the wedding day approached, I began to get cold feet. Damian was all for it. He had no idea it was a trick to get him under my father's control." She swallowed. "He was so happy, so blissfully unaware."

The muscle in Dom's jaw flexed, but he didn't interrupt.

"We flew out to a resort in the Caribbean for the wedding. It was the perfect setting. It should have been idyllic, and yet I was so wracked with guilt, I couldn't focus on what should have been the happiest day of my life."

"You married him?" Dom blurted out. "You went through with it?"

Her eyes filled with tears. "Yes. I promised to love and obey him in front of our friends and family, and then two days later, I ran away."

"Ran away? How? Where did you go?"

"I just took off."

Her heart twisted painfully in her chest. "Damian never saw it coming. We were out snorkeling, and I said I was going back to the hotel for a massage. Of course, that was a lie. I went straight to our room, packed my bag, then caught a cab to the airport. I left on the first plane back to the United States and never saw Damian again."

CHAPTER 19

Well, fuck me.

This woman never stopped surprising him.

"Are you still married?" Dom asked.

She shook her head. "No, Damian divorced me a few years later. A private investigator tracked me down and served the papers—I signed them without a second thought."

"He didn't come himself?" Dom couldn't believe the hacker had let her go so easily. If she was his woman... He shook his head.

Better not go there.

"No. I think he was too angry, or upset, or both. Alek found me, though. Told him I wasn't coming back, didn't want anything to do with him. He said Damian had disappeared, and no one knew where he was. I think my father tracked me down because he figured Damian might've tried to reach out, but he didn't."

Dom frowned. "That's why you and your father stopped talking?"

It was starting to add up now. The bastard used her. Used

his own daughter to keep a hacker in line. What a goddamn piece of shit.

"Yeah. We didn't speak again—until recently. I don't know what happened to Damian, but I carry the guilt around with me everywhere."

"It wasn't your fault." Dom felt the anger rise in his chest. "You were a kid. Your father used you."

"I know, but it doesn't make me feel any better."

They stood in silence as the sun gave one last valiant effort to shine, then sank into the ocean. It should have been a peaceful setting, but Ghost felt anything but. Inside, he was seething. He wanted to break Markov's face, pay him back for what he did to Becca, what he was still doing to her...

But when he glanced at her sad expression, his gut twisted.

Did she still have feelings for the hacker? Was that why she hadn't settled down? Or was she so messed up from it all that no one stood a chance? Easier to stay on the move than commit.

Yeah, he knew how that worked.

"Why'd you agree to work for him?" Ghost asked, once the sun was gone. "Why go through all this again?"

She sighed. "I didn't plan to. But when I ran into Alek at the embassy, something changed. He looked... older. More human. I thought maybe we could finally put the past to rest. He waited for me outside after work, convinced me to come work for him. Said he was making a fresh start here. Wanted to start over, make things right."

"And?"

She shook her head. "Nope. Same old bullshit. He never wanted to make amends. He just needed someone he could trust to help him set up shop and run his house. I'd done it before in San Francisco, so he knew he could count on me. I fell for it. Again. But he did offer a fat salary, more like a bribe, honestly." She sniffed. "At least he didn't lie about that."

"Then leave," Ghost said, his voice low and firm. "Take the money, get the hell out. Go back to the States and cut ties with this mess. Your father's not gonna save your ass when it all goes south. You'll be on your own. And for what? Loyalty to that bastard?"

She nodded miserably. "I know. I was just hoping it would be different this time."

Ghost grabbed her hand. "Listen to me, Becca. I'm going to try to get Markov at the delivery in Cartagena, three days from now. I told him this ambush spooked the cartel, and they want him there for reassurance. I think he's buying it."

She stared at him, not catching on.

"That's when the FBI will strike," he said. "If they get him there, caught in the act, he's done. No more hiding behind shell companies or fake names."

"Three days," she whispered, letting his words sink in.

He nodded. "The shipment's already moving. We've got no hard evidence connecting him to the deals. No paper trail, no weapon transfers in his name—he's too smart for that. We've got nothing else."

"I had a feeling something like this would happen," she admitted. "I just thought I'd have more time."

"Time's up," he said, his tone hardening. "You need to leave by tomorrow. Don't wait around for the authorities to arrive. You don't want to get tied up in any of this. With your history—"

She stared at him, horrified. "You mean with Damian?"

He shrugged. "Hacking, anonymous dealings on the dark web, and now arms dealing. It's going to be tough to prove you didn't know about any of this."

"Oh, God." She closed her eyes, the reality dawning. He didn't want to hurt her, but it was time she took her head out of the sand. Markov was going down, whether she liked it or not.

"Make sure to wipe your laptop. Get rid of anything that can link back to you."

She gulped, her eyes widening. "This is serious, isn't it?"

"It's life-in-prison serious."

He saw her knuckles go white as she gripped the railing.

"There's no other way?"

"He's gotta pay for what he's done, Becca. Either you get out, or you go down with him."

"Then, I'll leave tomorrow," she whispered, tears brimming in her eyes.

He gave a sharp nod, feeling some relief. At least she'd be safe. The FBI wouldn't come for her, wouldn't dig into her past. But as he looked at her, that relief started to twist into something bitter.

Once she left, he knew he'd never see her again.

Becca must have thought the same thing, because her honeyed gaze turned to him. The longing he saw there made his breath hitch.

"Can we be together tonight?" she whispered. "One last time?"

Fuck.

This was a really bad idea, but goddamn, he wanted her too.

Needed her.

One last night to savor her, cherish her, make her his own. One last night with the woman of his dreams.

Ghost helped her to her feet, and wordlessly led her back to his cabin.

CHAPTER 21

Becca stood in the bedroom, her heart racing as she watched Dom move toward her. The reality of the situation had hit her like one of the pounding waves she could still hear outside on the beach.

Tomorrow, she'd be gone. There was no avoiding it. No second chances. She'd leave him, and everything between them would become a memory.

But right now, here in this moment, he was still hers.

Her eyes traced the hard lines of his face, the stubbly shadow that covered his jaw, his soft lips and that low-burn in his eyes. She wanted to memorize every detail, every inch of him, commit it to memory so she could unpack it later, when she was alone.

He reached for her, sending a shiver down her spine. Her heart swelled as she moved into his arms. She didn't know how she felt about him, only that he affected her in a way no man ever had.

Ghost could see it, too. He didn't have to say anything. It was all there in his eyes—those dark, intense eyes that made her feel things she hadn't felt in years.

"Are you sure?" His voice was low, almost rough. Like he was offering her one last out, even though they both knew what was about to happen.

She nodded, her throat too tight to speak. Words would ruin this. Words would make it too real. Right now, she just wanted to feel—feel him, feel this moment—and forget about what was waiting on the other side of dawn.

When his lips met hers, it wasn't like before. This kiss was slower, softer. No urgency they'd shared in the past, just a sense of savoring the moment.

His hands moved over her back, drawing her closer until their bodies crushed together, heat building between them.

She felt like she was falling—into him, into this moment—and she didn't want to stop. Not yet.

She was breathless when he broke away. Slowly, he undressed her, slipping the dress off her shoulders and leaving it to sink with a soft sigh around her ankles.

His heated gaze roamed over her body, making her tremble with anticipation. It spoke of all the things he wanted to do to her, that he was going to do to her, before they parted ways tomorrow.

Then, he undressed, peeling off his shirt, then tugging down his cargo pants, never once taking his eyes off her. Her stomach tightened as desire swept through her body. When he pulled her down onto the bed, she was so ready for him.

A soft sigh escaped her as he ran a hand over her curves. "You're so goddamn beautiful," he muttered, and she could see by his eyes that he meant it. Then he lowered his head and kissed her. A deep, sensual kiss, nothing like the frenzied moment they'd had before. There was nothing rushed about this. He explored her mouth, savored her taste, as if they had all the time in the world.

But they didn't—that was the part that stung the most.

She traced the ridges of his back, memorizing the feel of

him—the solid strength of his body, the way his muscles flexed beneath her touch. He felt so good.

Real. Hard.

All man.

Breaking away, he kissed his way lower, leaving a hot trail across her feverish skin to her breast. When he sucked her nipple into his mouth, she felt the heat all the way to her core. Her eyes fluttered closed, and she arched her back as delicious sensations spread through her body.

She heard a moan and realized it was coming from her. That was a first. She'd never been a moaner, but Dom made her feel things nobody else did, and she couldn't help herself.

He moved his attention to her other breast, and she couldn't contain herself anymore. Reaching out, she buried her hands in his hair, pulling him toward her.

"Easy," he murmured, between gentle tugs on her nipple. "There's no rush. I want to enjoy you."

Except he was driving her crazy. She writhed against him, helpless and overwhelmed by emotion.

Eventually, he took pity on her, and lifted his head, or maybe it was because he couldn't contain himself any longer.

"You're driving me crazy," he murmured, as he lowered himself onto her.

She was driving him crazy?

Then, she felt his enormous hard-on prodding her and gulped. Okay, maybe he wasn't kidding.

Wrapping her arms around his neck, she pulled him closer, and his lips returned to hers, kissing her like she was the only thing that mattered. It was slow, deliberate, despite his obvious agony, and it made her chest tighten with emotions she didn't have words for.

God, she didn't want this to end.

But it had to.

They had to make every moment count.

A tear slid down her cheek, but she didn't bother to wipe it away. She didn't want him to see, but she couldn't stop the emotions that were crashing down around her. The tenderness, the pain of leaving, the fear that after tonight, she'd never feel anything like this again.

Dom lifted his head, his eyes meeting hers. For a moment, it was like time froze. The room went still, and all she could hear was the sound of their breathing, heavy and uneven. His hand came up, gently brushing her hair back from her face.

"It's okay," he whispered, his voice rough with emotion.

Her chest tightened at his words, and she bit her lip, trying to keep from crying.

She tried to hush the voice in her head that said it wasn't okay. It would never be okay again.

She didn't want to cry. Not now. Not when this was supposed to be their last perfect moment together.

"Sorry," she whispered, gazing up at him. He answered her with another searing kiss, this one she felt all the way to her toes. It left her feeling even more broken.

This wasn't just about sex. It wasn't about the heat between them or the physical need to be close. This was about something deeper. Something that scared the hell out of her because it was too real, too raw, too overwhelming.

She wasn't ready to put a name to it yet, but it was there, burning a hole in her chest. Leaving him tomorrow was going to rip her apart, but that was her secret to keep.

Slick with need and want, she lifted her hips off the bed to give him access, and with a low, almost pained groan, he slid into her.

"Fuck, Becca."

He dipped his head as the sensation took hold, and she felt his breath hitch. He wasn't the only one. She gasped along with him, as every fiber ignited. Every inch of him felt perfect, like they were made to fit together.

Her body arched toward him, her fingers digging into his back as he filled her utterly and completely. If she could capture one moment of their time together, this would be it.

Then he began to move.

Oh, holy hell!

Slow, unrushed, he thrust into her again, and her heart swelled as the familiar tightness in her belly grew. The pressure built surprisingly fast, for such a slow, sensual movement, but he didn't rush. It was like he too was cherishing every stroke, every spark that flew through their bodies as the tension mounted.

She opened her eyes and saw the agonized bliss on his face, and it sent her soaring higher and higher, until she reached breaking point. Soon, she was gasping with every thrust, clinging to him, desperately raising up to meet every stroke. Her body was on fire, an inferno of sweet, mind-blowing desire.

"Dom," she gasped, unsure what to do with the chaos of emotions spirally through her, crushing her with their intensity. Wrecking her so she would never be the same again.

She didn't want it to end, but holy crap, she was going to come in a hot, molten mess beneath him.

Right now!

She cried out as the first wave hit, wild and luxurious, a complete sensory overload. Then came the next one, and the next, until she didn't think she could bear it anymore. Some time, as she was convulsing around him, she thought she might have screamed his name, but she wasn't sure. All she knew, was as her body locked down, she heard him emit a ragged growl as he let go.

Another rush of feeling as he came—hard. His whole body tensed as he surged against her, his fingers fisting in her hair, his body damp with sweat. Like they were fused together in one ecstatic moment. She'd never felt closer to anyone.

Her legs clenched around his waist, as she dissolved around him, floating just this side of consciousness. He pulsed inside her until he was wrung dry, and then he collapsed, slick and spent.

Becca felt his heavy, masculine weight pressing down on her, his heart pounding next to hers—and she knew that nothing would ever be the same again.

CHAPTER 20

*G*host lay there, staring up at the dark ceiling, Becca's soft breath warming his chest.

What the hell had he done?

That was crazy, insane, completely off-the-scale good, and there was no rule book for this one. He was in enemy territory now, unsure of his way, relying on gut instinct alone to see him through.

Becca lay spent in his arms, her dark hair falling over his shoulder, her breathing even and rhythmic. He'd never seen anyone more angelic.

His chest tightened as he gazed down at her, feeling her breath on his chest. Fuck, how was he going to let her go?

Before tonight, this thing between them had been simple —manageable, at least. He could handle it. He'd been fully prepared to walk away when it was over, move on.

Now? Now, he wasn't so sure.

It was like something had shifted, something irreversible. A line had been crossed and there was no going back. He didn't even know what the hell it was. But it was something.

Something that felt like it might've just wrecked him for good.

He'd never been with anyone like Becca before. The way she'd taken him in, the way she'd wrapped herself around him—tight, warm, perfect—had left him raw and vulnerable. When she screamed his name, it had shredded him.

She wasn't just in his arms, she was in his damn head, in his soul. It was terrifying.

What the hell was he supposed to do with that?

She was his now. He knew it.

She might be leaving, but tonight, she'd given herself to him in a way that went beyond anything he'd ever felt. And, God help him, he'd given himself to her, too. There was no hiding behind the walls he'd spent years building up. No more undercover roles or bullshit lies. She'd seen him—really seen him.

And she still wanted him.

That's what killed him the most.

Her fingers trailed down his chest, her eyes closed, her face angelic. He couldn't remember ever feeling so close to another person. They'd made a connection, something real and solid, like a bond he didn't know he needed. But as much as he wanted to hold onto it, keep her close, he'd have to let her go.

She was leaving.

After tomorrow, he'd never see her again.

Something inside him twisted, made his chest tight.

Fuck.

He was going to let the best thing to ever happen to him walk out of his life, and that was that. She'd start over somewhere, build a new life—one he wasn't part of.

He didn't know what was in store for him. His future was a damn question mark. Always had been. But one thing he knew for sure—whatever it was, it didn't include her.

It couldn't.

Becca deserved better than this mess of a life he lived.

He glanced down at her, and his heart clenched. She'd told him she wanted something more—something stable. She wanted to settle down, maybe have a family. Hell, she wanted to be happy, and Ghost knew he couldn't give that to her. He didn't even know what happiness looked like anymore.

She needed more than a guy like him. More than a soldier without a mission. More than a man who lived on the edge, surviving undercover jobs, playing a game where any wrong move could get him killed.

What kind of future was that for her?

She'd been right—there was no happily ever after for people like him. That was a damn fairytale, one that didn't fit the brutal reality he lived in. He was a weapon, pure and simple, good for taking down scumbags, for infiltrating criminal organizations, but for love? For a family? That wasn't in the cards.

So why did he hate the idea of letting her go so much?

He kissed her head again, this time letting his lips linger, trying to memorize the feel of her, the way her body molded perfectly into his. His chest tightened again, that same damn ache that told him he was in too deep.

And he was. Too deep to walk away from this without feeling like he was leaving a part of himself behind.

But tomorrow would come. And when it did, she'd be gone, and he would go back to being who he was before her—a man built for survival, not love.

He just wished it didn't hurt so damn much.

WHEN BECCA finally drifted into a deep sleep, Ghost slipped out of bed as quietly as a shadow. Her soft breathing filled the room, chestnut hair spilling across the pillow, peaceful and completely unaware of the storm churning inside him.

For a second, he stood there, just looking at her. God, he didn't deserve her. Not with what was about to go down. But that was his world, wasn't it? Smoke and mirrors. Lies on top of lies. He clenched his jaw and forced himself to move.

Ghost crept across the room to the wardrobe, where he kept his military backpack stashed. His hands moved swiftly, silently, like second nature. Hidden in the lining, he found what he was looking for—the burner phone. The one that no one else knew about, not even Becca. He glanced back to make sure she hadn't stirred. Still sleeping. Still beautiful.

He slid out the door and tiptoed downstairs, keeping his movements light. Outside, the night air hit him, cool and salty. He crouched by the back deck and quickly tapped out a message to Pat, sending a pin-drop a little farther down the beach, outside the hacienda's boundaries. It wasn't ideal, but if they were going to meet, it had to be far enough away to avoid suspicion. Especially with the heat they were dealing with right now.

He knew it'd take Pat a while to get here. The guy was lounging in a cushy four-star hotel back in Panama City. Meanwhile, Ghost was neck-deep in enemy territory, trying to juggle a half-dozen lies without getting them all shot.

Again.

An hour later, his phone buzzed—Pat's reply.

Ghost checked on Becca one last time, making sure she was still dead to the world, then set off down the beach. He stuck to the shadows, hugging the line where the forest met the sand. His mind was running a mile a minute, but his movements stayed sharp, practiced. He couldn't afford to slip up, not now. Not this close to the endgame.

Twenty-five minutes later, he reached the meeting spot.

The only sound was the ocean, quiet and rhythmic. He scanned the area, listening, watching, until a low whistle cut through the night. Ghost whistled back, and Pat stepped out of the trees, blending in like he was part of the damn scenery.

Ghost grinned, despite himself. "Still got it, huh?"

Pat smirked, extending a hand. "Old habits, brother."

They shook hands, and Ghost gestured for them to sit on a fallen tree. They positioned themselves so they could watch each other's backs. It was second nature now—always watching, always expecting a threat. Hell, after everything they'd seen, they'd be fools not to.

"What's going on?" Pat asked, his tone casual, but Ghost could hear the edge underneath. He wasn't a fan of surprises. None of them were.

He got straight to the point. "There was an ambush. We've got a leak. Someone's feeding intel, and it's screwing with the operation."

Pat frowned, eyes narrowing. "Any idea who?"

Ghost shook his head. "Been running through every name. No one makes sense. But someone's talking."

"The Panamanians?"

Ghost exhaled through his nose. "Can't trust them. Too risky to ask questions that'd raise flags. We keep digging, we'll tip our hand. There is... one other possibility, though."

Pat's eyebrow shot up. "I'm listening."

"Ramirez's wife. They've been having problems for months. She called Becca the other night—really upset. We think she may have been the leak."

"Can we confirm it?"

Ghost's jaw tightened. "No. She's dead. Freak car accident yesterday—on her way to the airport."

Pat didn't miss a beat. "That's convenient."

"Too convenient."

Pat drummed his fingers on his thigh, thinking. "I'll check it out. We've got contacts who can run her phone records, see if anything stands out."

"Do it. But at this point, it's secondary. The shipment's already with my contact on the Colombian side. He's holding it until we give the green light."

"When's the drop?"

"The day after tomorrow. I'm flying out to Bogotá tomorrow to oversee it. You wanna tag along?"

A grin split Pat's face. "Wouldn't miss it for the world. Nothing like a good showdown to make things interesting."

Ghost chuckled, but it was short-lived. He still had one more bomb to drop, and he knew Pat wasn't gonna like it.

"There's... a complication," he said, his tone shifting.

Pat's grin faded. "What kind of complication?"

Ghost dragged a hand over his face. "Becca. She's not just Markov's assistant... she's his daughter."

Pat blinked, staring at him for a long moment before leaning in, his voice low. "How much does she know?"

"About her father? Not much. About me? Everything."

"Shit, Ghost." Pat's face twisted in frustration. "You've been sleeping with Markov's daughter?"

He didn't bother with excuses. Pat would see through him in a heartbeat. "She's back at my place right now."

Pat swore under his breath. "Do you trust her? What if she tells him who you really are? She'll blow the whole fucking op wide open."

"She won't," he said firmly, ignoring the tight knot in his gut. "She's leaving tomorrow. I told her to get out, that it's not safe. Once we grab Markov, everything's gonna go sideways. I can't risk her being around for that."

Pat gave him a long, hard look, then sighed. "You better be right, man. If she doesn't leave..."

"She will," Ghost cut in, his voice steady. He had to believe it. "I'll make damn sure she does."

"Good." Pat rubbed the back of his neck, exhaling sharply. "We can't afford loose ends. Once the fireworks start, no one's safe. You know that better than anyone."

He nodded, feeling the weight of it pressing down on him. There were too many loose ends already. But Becca... she wasn't part of this world. She shouldn't have to deal with the fallout.

He needed to get her out, keep her safe. Even if it meant never seeing her again.

"In the meantime," Ghost said, shifting back into mission mode, "get in touch with your contacts. We need every piece in place. I'll send you the coordinates and the time of the handover when I have them."

Pat gave him a curt nod. "I'm on it. After the Suarez bust, the higher-ups are all over us. They're ready for round two."

Ghost nodded. That was Pat's domain—the bureaucrats and suits. Ghost's job was simple. Get Markov to the drop. Catch him red-handed. And get Becca the hell out of dodge before the whole thing went nuclear.

The two men sat there in silence for a minute, listening to the waves. There was a quiet understanding between them, the kind only men like them could share. They'd been through enough ops to know how this would play out. They'd catch Markov, take down his empire. And then? Then it was back to the grind, back to the shadows.

And Becca... Becca would be gone.

Ghost shook his head, pushing the thought away. There was no room for sentimentality in this line of work. Not when lives were at stake. He'd done what he could for her. Now it was up to her to listen.

"You better book that flight," he said, standing up. "I'll see you in Bogotá."

Pat stood and clapped him on the back. "Take care, Ghost. Watch your six."

Ghost nodded, his mind already shifting back to Becca, to what the next 48 hours would bring. "Always."

CHAPTER 23

"Where'd you get to?" Becca asked as Dom climbed back into bed. His skin was cool to the touch, and he smelled of the sea and the sand.

"I couldn't sleep, so I went for a walk."

She wrapped herself around him, sharing her warmth, pressing her body against his. "You should've told me. I'd have come with you."

"Didn't want to wake you." He pulled her closer, his arms encircling her waist. The quiet strength in his touch always grounded her, made her feel safe. Safe in a way she hadn't felt in a long time. Possibly ever.

After everything they'd been through, after the way they'd connected earlier, she felt closer to him than ever. Like she could be herself, fully. Like he *saw* her, all of her, and didn't turn away.

It still hurt that this was going to be their last night together, but she pushed that thought aside, buried it deep, because tonight was about them. She wasn't ready to say goodbye just yet.

Tonight, she wanted to lose herself in him—*all* of him.

She wanted to feel him, touch him, taste him. She wanted to explore every part of him while she still had the chance.

Lying on top of him, she kissed the side of his neck, her lips grazing his skin, moving slowly, savoring the moment. His low hum of approval vibrated against her lips, sending warmth through her. Smiling, she trailed kisses down his chest, letting her tongue dart out every so often to taste him. His scent, the salty tang of the ocean still clinging to him, filled her senses.

Dom's hand grasped her hair, gently guiding her down as her kisses moved lower. She followed the trail of dark hair down his chest, past his stomach, kissing every inch of skin along the way.

He was already aroused, and she took a moment to appreciate the entire glorious length of him. She doubted she'd ever experience anything so fine again.

He gazed at her—*ready*, his breath already coming in shallow huffs, even though they were only getting started.

With a teasing flick of her tongue, she licked the length of him and heard him curse under his breath. His hands tightened in her hair. Emboldened, she took him into her mouth, moving slowly at first, her hand following the same rhythm. She wasn't in any hurry, not this time. She wanted to enjoy this—enjoy *him*.

"Fuck, Becca," he growled, his head falling back, eyes closing as she worked him deeper. She loved the sound of his voice, that rough, ragged edge that always came when he lost control.

His muscles tensed beneath her hands, his body reacting to every move she made, and it gave her a sense of power—knowing she could do this to him, that she could make him unravel with just a touch.

It wasn't like the first time, when it had been fast and

frantic, or the last time, when they'd clung to every moment afraid it might be their last. This was different.

It was slow. Intentional. It was about enjoying the moment, relishing every erotic sensation.

Becca moaned softly against him, and his hips lifted off the bed as he pushed deeper into her mouth. His hands fisted in her hair, but he wasn't rough, just desperate, his breath coming faster, harsher.

"Shit, Becca... I—" He cut himself off with another groan, and she smiled, loving the way he was falling apart beneath her.

But before she could take him any further, Dom grabbed her shoulders and flipped her over, pinning her beneath him. She gasped, the sudden shift taking her by surprise, but it only lasted a moment before his mouth was on hers, kissing her deeply, hungrily, as if he couldn't get enough.

Her heart pounded in her chest as his hands roamed her body, teasing her skin, exploring her curves with a reverence that made her breath hitch. His touch was firm, but gentle, as if he was rediscovering every inch of her, and she melted into it, into *him*.

"You drive me crazy," he rasped against her lips, his voice thick with want. "Now it's my turn."

Becca barely had time to breathe before his lips were trailing down her body, leaving a path of fire in their wake. When his mouth found its place between her legs, she gasped and clutched the sheets beside her. His tongue moved over her with an agonizing slowness, each stroke deliberate, drawing every ounce of her pleasure from within. Each flick, every tease, felt like a promise—a slow burn that made her toes curl and her body arch toward him.

"Oh, God," she moaned, her back arching off the bed. He was taking his time, drawing her out, bringing her close to the edge, only to pull back before she could tip over.

It was maddening and delicious all at once, and she loved it. Loved the way he was making her feel, loved the way he was *playing* with her.

She was lost in the sensations, her body a trembling mess beneath him, and still, he didn't let up. His tongue moved with precision, his lips teasing her, sucking just hard enough to make her gasp, to make her squirm under his touch.

The tension coiled inside her, like a wave threatening to crash over her, but he kept her there, hovering on the brink, making her whimper with need.

"Dom... please..." she begged, her voice a coarse whisper. She was so close, so ready, but he wasn't letting her fall.

Finally, after what felt like an eternity, he released her, moving up her body until his face was hovering over hers. His eyes were dark, intense, and filled with something that made her breath catch in her throat. He didn't say anything, but the look was enough to make her heart race.

You ready? he seemed to be asking, his gaze locking with hers.

She nodded, her hands gripping his shoulders, pulling him closer.

Hell, yeah.

She'd never been more ready.

He smiled, that slow, sexy smile that always made her knees weak, and positioned himself at her entrance. The anticipation was almost too much—her whole body trembled with need, every nerve was on fire.

She *wanted* this moment, wanted to feel him, all of him.

When he finally slid into her, she gasped, her fingers digging into his skin as he filled her completely. The sensation was overwhelming, a mix of pleasure and pressure that had her head spinning.

He began to move, slowly, deliberately, his eyes never

leaving hers as he thrust deeper, pushing her closer and closer to the edge with every movement.

Her body was so primed, so ready, that it didn't take long before she was right there again, teetering on the brink.

And this time, when the wave hit, it hit hard.

Her entire body tensed, her muscles tightening around him as her orgasm crashed over her, pulling her under, drowning her in sensation.

"Dom!" Her voice broke as the pleasure consumed her. He wasn't far behind, his own release hitting him with a deep, guttural groan that sent a shiver down her spine. She felt him shudder inside her, his body tensing as he found his own release, and knowing he was coming too, sent her flying even higher.

They stayed like that for a moment, both of them breathing hard, their bodies still tangled together, hearts racing.

Eventually, she let out a soft, contented sigh as she basked in the afterglow. This wasn't just sex anymore. It hadn't been for a while.

This was them. Together.

Even though she knew this was the end, that tomorrow they'd be going their separate ways, right now, in this moment, she didn't care.

Because tonight, they had each other.

And that was enough.

CHAPTER 21

Becca's hands shook as she gripped the bathroom sink, staring into the mirror. The paleness of her face, the slight tremble in her lip—it didn't do justice to the storm ripping through her chest.

She'd run before.

Hell, was no stranger at slipping away, vanishing into the folds of the world when things got too heated.

But this? This was different.

She wasn't running from a relationship that had turned toxic or a situation she wanted to get out of, she was running from the man she loved.

Oh, Dom.

Her heart squeezed painfully at the thought of walking away, especially after the night they'd had. Could she do this?

His words snapped her back to reality.

Leave your laptop behind. Destroy your SIM card.

It was serious this time. No half-measures, no turning back. The authorities weren't just sniffing around—they were coming.

If she stayed, it wouldn't be long before she was staring at the grimy walls of a Panamanian jail cell. She squeezed her eyes shut, hoping the panic would recede, taking deep breaths that barely steadied her nerves.

She turned on the shower, mentally running through the plan again. Pack, taking nothing that wouldn't fit in her shoulder bag. Go to work as usual, acting normally. While she was there, she'd wipe her laptop and get rid of any hint of her presence. This afternoon, she'd come up with some excuse to head into town where she'd kill her cellphone and draw emergency cash.

Then get to the airport.

Simple, right?

Her thoughts turned to Chrissy, who'd been doing exactly the same thing when she was killed. An icy chill swept over her.

She had to be so careful. Chrissy was Ramirez's wife, while she—Becca—was nobody to him. If he thought she was a liability...

Surely her father wouldn't sanction—?

It didn't bear thinking about.

God, she wasn't ready to leave. Not like this. Not with everything hanging in the balance. But what choice did she have? The clock was ticking, and the situation was closing in around her.

Then she remembered Fernando.

Shit, she had to warn him. The last thing she wanted was to drag him or the other staff into this mess. Her life was crumbling, but she wouldn't let innocent people be caught in the crossfire. They didn't deserve that.

She stepped under the water, hoping it would wash away the fear and the anxiety. The suds twisted down the drain, carrying the scent of Dom with them. She watched the bubbles disappear, and it hit her how final this was.

That last piece of him, gone.

Becca took a ragged breath. This was not the time to get emotional. Sentimentality was a luxury she couldn't afford.

She could fall apart later, sob on the plane, or bury her head in a pillow once she was miles away. Right now, she had to hold it together.

She scrubbed her skin harder, determined to wash away the emotional grime as easily as the dirt.

This was happening, and she had to get herself together. Stepping out, she felt marginally more in control. She dried herself off, dressed in comfortable clothes and flat shoes, nothing that would draw attention. Outside, the sun was blazing down. It was going to be another scorching day. Already, the air was heavy with heat, the kind that pressed down on your shoulders, but that could be the anxiety.

She'd have to ask Carlos for a lift. That's what made this so nerve-wracking. Would he know something was up? Would he sense something had changed in her?

Everything had to look totally normal. She couldn't take anything with her. Blinking back tears, Becca walked around the room one last time, touching the things she knew she had to leave behind. Scarves, beads from the market, handmade dishes from that charming little village, her favorite shawl—the vibrant red and gold one she wrapped around herself on colder nights.

All of it had to stay. If she took anything, Carlos would know she was running.

Alek would come after her, she knew that.

When she wasn't there to meet Carlos for her pickup, they'd launch a search party. The first place they'd look would be the airport. If she wasn't quick, they'd find her before she even made it past security.

Becca stood in the center of the room, her heart aching at the thought of leaving her little collection of memories behind. But that was just it—memories were all they could be now. Tangible reminders of a life that no longer fit her, not when her very freedom was on the line.

"There'll be time for more later," she thought, but the words didn't lessen the sting.

She grabbed her bag and passport, mentally checking off each item on her list. The most painful thing was the one she couldn't physically pack. She'd wanted more from her father. Always had. But deep down, she knew he'd never be the man she needed him to be. Dom had helped her realize that. No matter how much she loved Alek, or how many times she hoped things would be different, he just was not capable. He'd pull her down with him if she let him.

As much as it hurt, she wasn't going to be collateral damage in his mess.

Not this time.

It was time to let go. And that terrified her more than anything else.

BECCA WAS at her desk promptly at nine a.m. She forced a smile when Alek strode into the office, his presence filling the room like a dark cloud.

"Morning," she chirped, keeping her voice light.

"Becca, I need you to book me, Ramirez, and Dominguez on a flight to Bogotá this evening," he said, not even glancing in her direction as he headed straight for his study. "And book the light aircraft to fly us to Cartagena first thing tomorrow morning."

Her stomach flipped. So, Dom had actually convinced him. The handover of the merchandise to the cartel was happening. She swallowed, struggling to keep her voice even. "How long will you be staying?"

"Two days," he replied curtly.

"Same hotel?"

He nodded, unlocking the door to his office and tucking the key into his jacket pocket. "And bring me my tea," he added, disappearing inside.

Typical. No "good morning," no "thank you." Nothing. Just commands.

Becca bit the inside of her cheek, her exhaustion clawing at her. She'd barely slept, her mind whirling with plans and panic, but she had to stay focused.

Had to act normal.

She delivered his tea, then sat back at her desk to book their flights. As she typed in Dominguez's name, her chest tightened. They were about to go in completely different directions—him to danger, and her to a slim chance of safety. She thought back to the previous night, the way he'd held her, his solid arms wrapped around her like a shield, but not even he could protect her from the storm that was fast approaching. The memory of his touch still lingered, but it was fading, just like everything else she had hoped for.

Casting off the sadness, she turned back to the screen. With the booking website still open, she pulled up a list of flights to the United States.

Plenty of options leaving today.

She chewed her lower lip. Should she book one now? It would be easy, just a few clicks. No, it was too risky. If anyone checked with the airline, they'd know. Better to buy the ticket in person, leaving no trace.

Starting at the top of her mental checklist, she wiped her internet search history, cleared the cookies, deleted her stored passwords. Her fingers moved quickly, erasing everything personal from her hard drive. She switched her username to something generic, though she knew the authorities could recover whatever they wanted with the right tools. Just in case, she wiped down the laptop, her pulse steadying slightly as her fingerprints disappeared from its surface.

With that done, she headed out to find Carlos. She hated having to ask permission to go into town, but it was the only way out. She also needed him to arrange transportation for Alek and the others to the airport.

"Sanchez will take you," Carlos said without looking up from his paperwork. "I'm busy with the boss."

Becca nodded. "Fine." Even better. She wouldn't have him leering all over her.

Her next stop was the kitchen, where Fernando was whisking eggs, his arm a blur of motion. When he saw her, he stopped.

"Hi, Becca. Is it time for the boss's lunch already?"

"No." She glanced around. "It's not."

He frowned, sensing something off. "What's wrong?"

She dropped her voice. "Remember when you told me to let you know if trouble was coming?"

His eyes narrowed, concern deepening the lines on his face. "Si."

"Well," she hesitated, "it's coming."

Fernando's face darkened. "Is it the police? Or… criminales?"

"The police." She studied his reaction. Why would he jump to criminals first?

He nodded solemnly. "When?"

"Two days. Maybe less."

He sighed, a weary sound. "I knew this day would come."

"How did you know?" Curiosity momentarily outweighing her fear.

He shrugged. "Look around. This place is guarded like a fortress, but Panama isn't that dangerous. Besides, people talk. The boss has a reputation. A very bad one."

Becca swallowed hard. Of course, Fernando knew more than she'd realized. She squeezed his hand, feeling the roughness of his palm. "Be safe, Fernando. Tell the others."

"Gracias, Senorita. You too."

With a heavy heart, she turned and left the kitchen.

As she crossed the hallway, Alek came out of his office, frowning at the stain on his blazer. The door locked automatically behind him. "I've spilled tea on this. Can you have one of the staff take care of it before I leave tonight?"

"Of course," Becca replied, taking the blazer. She knew he meant *her*. There was no one else. Fernando was busy with the kitchen, and the maid had her hands full with the bedrooms. She handed Alek his printed tickets. "You're all checked in."

"Good," he muttered. "I've got to pack. I'll have lunch in my quarters."

"Okay," Becca nodded, watching him walk away. She was about to hang the blazer over her chair when something hard in the pocket caught her attention. Her fingers brushed against metal. She pulled it out and froze.

The keys to his office.

Becca stared at them for a long moment. Dom's words echoed in her brain. Look for evidence of the arms deal with the Colombians. Should she, or shouldn't she? The damn key was burning a hole in her hand. Time seemed to stand still as she tried to decide what to do. This might be the one chance she had to search his study, undetected. If she could find the evidence Dom needed, it would help them charge Alek and that brute Ramirez and bring down their gunrunning organization. He deserved it. She no longer thought of Alek as her father. It was quite clear she meant nothing to him. She'd been blind. Naive. Hoping for a relationship he wasn't capable of. With a final breath, she gave a firm nod. Now it was time to do the right thing. To be on the right side. Dom's side.

Glancing around, she saw the coast was clear. Her hand

trembled as she slid the key into the lock. The door clicked open, and she slipped inside, taking the keys with her.

She moved quickly, passing the bookcase and coffee table surrounded by four armchairs, and heading straight to his desk. She didn't bother with his laptop. It would be locked, and she didn't have time to crack passwords.

Her pulse raced as she opened the drawers. The first was neatly organized with pens and paper. Useless. The second made her pause—a gun, holstered, with spare bullets. She slammed it shut, her hands shaking.

In the third drawer, she found what she was looking for. A stack of documents. Becca's breath caught. It was all there —gun types, quantities, destinations. This was the deal with the Colombians, no doubt about it. Automatic rifles, rocket-propelled grenades, things she didn't even recognize.

She flipped to the last page, her heart hammering as her eyes scanned for a signature. But it wasn't Alek's. Or Ramirez's. Just a scribble, a name she didn't recognize.

Damn.

Still, it was something. She snapped pictures of the documents with her phone, then quickly returned everything to its place. Her pulse pounded in her ears as she padded back to the door, cracking it open just enough to peek out. The hallway was empty.

Just as she stepped out, a hard voice stopped her cold.

"What the hell are you doing?"

CHAPTER 22

Carlos.
She froze.

"Oh, I was just tidying up. Mr. Markov is leaving tonight, and I wanted to make sure everything was in order before he left."

Carlos narrowed his eyes. "I don't believe you. Mr. Markov doesn't let anyone in his office. Not even you." He spat the last words like venom.

"Honestly, he gave me the keys. Look." She held them up as proof, but her hand was trembling.

"There's one way to sort this out." He gripped her arm.

"Let me go, Carlos. I want to speak to my—— to Mr. Markov. Now."

"That will be arranged."

Without releasing her, he dragged her out of the office and into the hallway. She barely managed to keep her footing as he barked an order to one of the security guards. The guard nodded and hurried off, probably to inform Alek about what had happened.

"Where are you taking me?" she demanded, trying to pull away, but his grip only tightened.

He dragged her down a narrow corridor toward the storage and surveillance rooms. She didn't come here often and barely knew the layout. He stopped halfway, shoved open a door, and pushed her inside a small, musty storage room. "Stay here. Mr. Markov's on his way," he said, locking the door behind her.

Her heart sank. This was bad. Really bad. There was no talking her way out of this one.

Alek would be furious. She never cleaned his office, and everyone knew he was paranoid about people going in there without him.

Sighing, she sank down onto a creaky wooden chair and looked around. The room smelled faintly of chlorine from the pool equipment stored nearby. A few boxes were stacked in the corner, a vacuum cleaner leaning against the wall. How the hell was she going to get out?

Dom!

He hadn't left yet. Maybe he could still help. She fumbled for her phone, her fingers shaking, but her heart sank when she saw the single bar of reception. Barely anything. She tried sending a text, but it wouldn't go through.

Come on!

She tried again. Still nothing.

The heavy sound of footsteps echoed in the hall. She shoved her phone into her pocket just as the door opened, and Alek stepped in. He wasn't smiling.

"What's this about, Becca? Carlos says he caught you snooping in my study?" The pale blue eyes were cold and suspicious.

She swallowed. "Yes, I found your key in your jacket pocket, so I went in to have a look around." She may as well be honest—at least about that part. He'd see straight through a lie. "You've never told me what business you're in. I know it's not farming equipment."

He frowned.

"So I decided to see for myself." By the look on his face, she knew she'd hit a nerve. He'd never have admitted to his illegal activities because he didn't trust her.

He couldn't. She'd left him once before.

"You could have just asked me."

She fixed her gaze on him, defiant now. It was her only bluff out of here. "If I had, would you have told me the truth?"

He avoided the question. "What did you find?"

"Nothing," she lied smoothly. "Carlos came before I could really look around."

Alek stared at her, unblinking, then turned to Carlos. "Search her."

"Seriously? What—?"

Carlos entered the room, his face expressionless. He patted her down, rough hands grazing places they shouldn't, making her skin crawl.

"That's enough!" she snapped, stepping back.

Creep. He made her skin crawl.

He took her phone and handed it to Alek.

Markov handed her the device. "Open it."

"Why?"

"Open it, Becca."

She turned away. "No, it's my personal phone. It's got nothing to do with you."

Alek gave Carlos a subtle nod. Before she could react, Carlos backhanded her across the face. Pain exploded in her cheek, and she stumbled, gasping for breath.

"Open. It." Alek's voice was deadly calm.

With a sob, she held it up to her face, so it unlocked the screen. He snatched it from her hand, scrolling through the messages and photos. He grunted when there was nothing to find, then he searched through the photographs.

His expression darkened. "So, you did find something." He held the phone up so she could see what he was looking at.

Becca paled. This was going from bad to worse. She hadn't had time to delete the photographs, but at least she hadn't sent them to Dom. His cover was still intact.

"What were you planning to do with these, Becca?"

"Nothing. I told you, I just wanted to see what you were up to." She burst into tears, a mixture of fear and pent-up anger. "You never tell me anything."

Alek's expression didn't waver. He was unmoved by her tears.

He didn't care. He never had.

Dom had been right—her father wasn't capable of love. And Carlos, that brute, watched with a sick grin, enjoying her humiliation.

"Did you sabotage the shipment?" Alek's voice dropped to a growl.

"What shipment?" she asked, trying to keep her voice steady, but she knew what was coming.

He waved the phone in front of her face. "*This* one. Don't lie to me. You're smarter than you act. You found out about the shipment, didn't you? And you told someone. That's how the authorities knew."

"I didn't," she pleaded. "I would never do that to you!"

Alek's temper flared. "Then how did they know where to find us?" He kicked the leg of the chair, making it wobble. "Dominguez said there was a leak, but I didn't realize the leak was my own daughter."

Carlos gaped at them.

It was good to see him taken by surprise, even if it did

give him even more reason to hate her. Sure enough, his leer turned into a glower of disgust.

Alek's voice softened, but it wasn't with kindness. "I expected more from you, Rebecca. I should've known better. You and Damian—you're the same. You both deserted me." He snorted. "So much for family loyalty, huh?"

For a moment, Becca forgot to be afraid. "You used Damian! He wanted out and you wouldn't let him go. You manipulated me into marrying him to keep him under your control. It was a despicable thing to do."

If he was surprised at her retaliation, he didn't show it. "It was necessary."

Only to his criminal enterprise. He made her sick. She couldn't believe she'd spent all this time and energy trying to forge a bond with him. "Well, maybe you could live with that, but I couldn't."

They should have had this discussion months, if not years ago. If they had, she wouldn't even be here.

"I made that man what he is today," Alek sneered. "And how did he repay me? By disclosing all the dark web transactions to the goddamn Feds. What a rat!"

"He did what?"

She gaped at him, confused. Last she'd heard, Damian had disappeared, never to be seen again.

"Oh, didn't you know? Your darling ex-husband betrayed me to the Feds."

She stared at him, but Alek wasn't done. "He's a billionaire philanthropist, thanks to me. I funded his start-up when it was nothing more than an idea on a rebuilt laptop in my spare room. That boy had nowhere to go when I found him. He owes me everything!"

"I had no idea," Becca whispered, still amazed at what her ex had become. He'd always been brilliant—it was just a matter of time before he hit the big time. She was glad. After everything he'd been through, he deserved it.

"Backstabbing bastard."

"Is that why you're hiding out here in Panama?" Becca asked. "Because the Feds are after you?"

"He's the reason I had to leave America," Markov snarled. "My damn home! Now I'm stuck here in this cesspool of a jungle making deals with the goddamn cartels. It would be laughable, if it wasn't so fucking tragic."

Carlos shifted his feet as if to remind Alek he was still there.

It worked. Alek exhaled and threw her cell phone on the ground. It cracked, along with any chance of rescue. Then he stood on it, grinding his heel into it until it was well and truly broken—along with her dream of getting out of here.

Now there was no way to tell Dom she was in trouble.

She stifled a sob. "What are you going to do with me?"

"Me? Nothing. Carlos, on the other hand—"

He turned to his henchman, who's eyes flickered in anticipation. "Find out if she's told us everything."

CHAPTER 23

The plane from Panama City to Bogotá touched down just after 7:00 p.m. Markov and Ramirez hadn't said much during the hour-and-a-half flight, so Ghost had reclined his seat and dozed off. He hadn't got much sleep the night before, and small talk wasn't his thing.

The sprawling, high-altitude city was thriving when they arrived, despite the late hour. According to the chatty taxi driver, there was a ten-day flower festival starting tomorrow and everyone was in a party mode.

The drive to the hotel took an hour, thanks to the heavy traffic, and by the time they arrived, all Ghost wanted was a hot shower and a bed. Unfortunately, he knew sleep wasn't in the cards for a while.

He hadn't seen Becca all afternoon, which was probably for the best. She had gone into town like she'd planned, and by now, she was hopefully on her way to the U.S. There was no way to reach her, not since she'd destroyed her SIM card.

A pang of longing hit him out of nowhere.

Damned if he couldn't still see her in his mind, head

thrown back in ecstasy, eyes closed, lips parted, her soft body wrapped around his afterward.

He shook off the memory, irritated at the ache in his chest. He needed to get a grip. She'd only been gone a few hours. The feelings would fade eventually, but right now, it was like a raw wound.

And what the fuck was up with Markov and Ramirez? They hadn't said more than a few words to him the entire flight. Had something gone down between them? Markov barely acknowledged him as they reached the hotel.

"See you tomorrow," Markov snapped, heading for the elevator.

What? No dinner invite?

Fine by him. He wasn't interested in spending more time with scum like Markov anyway. Their relationship was strictly business—he was the fixer, the guy who moved the product. No friends, no pleasantries, and that's how he liked it.

One thing Ghost knew for sure was he did not trust Alek Markov or his slimy partner. Not one bit.

Tomorrow, they'd be taking a private plane to Cartagena for the handoff. The deal was happening at Miguel's farmhouse, or rather, the old sugarcane warehouse nearby that now served as storage for the goods. It was going to be a long day.

After a quick shower, Ghost changed into dark jeans and a black hoodie, something low-key. His hotel room was big, with a view of the sprawling city. Bogotá wasn't exactly beautiful, but it had character. Rich in culture, history, museums, and lately, a foodie scene. He ordered room service and shot a quick text to Pat. The night was far from over, and there was still plenty to get done.

At midnight, Ghost slipped down the service stairs and exited through a back door into the deserted alley behind the hotel. He could hear distant music and laughter from party-goers celebrating the festival. Sticking to the shadows, he made his way to their meeting point—a dive bar in one of the sketchier parts of town.

When he walked in, a band was butchering a classic rock song, and the few patrons left were either nursing their drinks or hoping to score with one of the bartenders, who didn't seem too picky if the price was right.

He spotted Pat sitting at a table in the back with two other men. Ghost recognized Blade from their first meeting, but the third guy was new.

"This is Cole," Pat said, nodding toward the tall guy with sandy blond hair.

"Good to meet you." Cole held out his hand.

Ghost shook it and nodded to Grant before sitting down. "Thanks for coming."

Pat wasted no time. "Give us the time of the handoff, and we'll be there early. I haven't looped in the Colombian authorities yet, for obvious reasons, but the FBI has got two agents waiting in Cartagena for my call."

Ghost nodded. "The deal's going down tomorrow at 7 p.m. We're flying out in the morning."

Pat nodded back. "We've got a light aircraft ready at a private airstrip outside the city. We'll be there before dawn." Ghost had already given them the location of Miguel's farm, but not the timing—until now.

Ghost leaned in, lowering his voice. "Listen, I don't trust this bastard. I want to set up some extra precautions."

Pat grinned, his eyes glinting. "I was hoping you'd say that. What do you have in mind?"

"What the hell—?"

Ghost sat up in bed as the door burst open and Alek

Markov stormed in, followed by Ramirez and three thugs from the hacienda.

What were they doing here?

By the looks on their faces, it wasn't good.

Then he knew.

Becca.

Two of the thugs grabbed him by the arms and hauled him out of bed, while the third punched him in the face and then again in the gut. He doubled over with a grimace. It wasn't the worst hit he'd taken, but it wasn't soft either.

"What the fuck is going on?" he snapped, glaring at Markov, who was scowling at him like he'd just murdered his best friend.

"This is what's going on," the arms dealer said coldly, holding up his phone.

Ghost's stomach twisted painfully as he stared at the screen. There was a picture of Becca tied to an old wooden chair in a concrete room. She'd been worked over. Her beautiful face was black and blue, one eye swollen shut. Her head hung forward, and blood dripped from her nose and mouth. She didn't look conscious.

He growled like a cornered animal, hot fury spreading through his veins. "How could you do that to your own daughter?" If looks could kill, Markov would be dying a slow death right now. "What kind of monster are you?"

"She betrayed me," Markov snarled. "As did you. Becca told Carlos everything."

Ghost balled his hands into fists. So, it was Carlos who'd done that to her. Just wait until he got hold of that scumbag. He was going to throttle the life out of him with his bare hands. Markov thought he was tough, just wait until he saw what damage Ghost could inflict.

"I know you work for the U.S. government, and you've

been screwing my daughter under my nose. Used her to get to me, huh?"

Ghost spat at Markov's feet. "No. She was for pleasure. I got to you all on my own."

Another punch landed, harder this time, sending stars flickering across Dom's vision.

"Easy," Ramirez warned. "We need him for the handover."

Ghost had purposely kept Markov in the dark about the details, making sure he'd be there when it all went down.

"It was you who set up Suarez, wasn't it?" Markov growled, obviously having figured a few things out, based on this new information. "He went down because of you."

Ghost managed a laugh, despite the ache in his jaw. "Wrong again. I was brought in after Suarez went down. The Feds saw an opportunity and took it. I work for the highest bidder."

He could tell Markov wasn't fully convinced, but if he wanted the arms dealer to show up at the handover, Ghost had to sell it.

"I don't believe him," Ramirez hissed. "He could have the cops waiting for us."

"Nobody, except me, knows where or when this is going down," Ghost gritted out. "Not even the buyers. They're waiting for me to text them the location."

There was a long pause as Markov considered his options.

Eventually, he held up his phone again, showing the picture of a battered Becca. "Just make sure you don't try anything, or you'll never see my daughter again."

CHAPTER 24

This was sugarcane country.

Ghost peered out of the small plane window at the landscape below. Endless cane fields stretched out, eventually swallowed by the rainforest. Through the dusky haze, he spotted the farmhouse where Miguel lived with his family, along with several other outhouses scattered across the sprawling property.

Miguel was a wealthy, well-respected farmer in these parts, but despite his subpar harvests, he still managed to provide a lavish lifestyle for his family. His real income didn't come from agricultural produce.

As they descended toward the dusty road that would serve as a landing strip, Ghost made out the large, semi-derelict barn on the edge of Miguel's property where the deal was set to go down. Surrounded on three sides by cane fields, there was nothing nearby for miles except the encroaching jungle.

From a distance, the barn looked abandoned, but closer inspection revealed its fortifications: a steel-reinforced door, boarded-up upper windows, and no back entrance. The place was a fortress.

Miguel, paranoid about his own safety and his family's, never attended these deals. Entry to the barn was controlled by a ten-digit code that had to be entered into a sophisticated security panel hidden behind a crooked wooden slat. Despite its rundown appearance, the barn had a state-of-the-art setup powered by an internal generator.

The Cessna's engine growled as they landed hard on the bumpy road, the wheels kicking up dirt and gravel. The plane rattled along the makeshift runway before coming to a stop.

"Follow me," Ghost said to the others, three of whom were armed, their fingers twitchy. One wrong move, and this would all go to hell.

Ghost led them to a beat-up pickup truck parked by the side of the road, its keys in the ignition.

"Someone should stay and watch the plane," he suggested.

It wasn't necessary—the pilot was being paid by the hour—but any chance to thin out their group was worth taking. One less gun to worry about.

Markov pointed at one of the thugs. "You. Stay here and guard the plane. Make sure the pilot stays put, no matter what. He's our ride out of here."

The thug nodded, his hand instinctively reaching for the weapon at his back.

Ghost wondered where the FBI agents and the Colombian authorities were hiding. He guessed they were camped out in the rainforest, which was less than a hundred meters from the barn and provided excellent cover. He already knew where Pat and the other Blackthorn Security operatives were; he'd given them the passcode yesterday before flying out.

"Any funny business, and your girlfriend gets a bullet to the head," Markov snarled, still as paranoid as ever. Ghost raised a hand in mock surrender.

They piled into the truck, with Markov sitting up front, gun trained on Ghost, and Ramirez in the back with the two thugs.

Ghost started the engine. "The barn's at the edge of the property. This is the only road there."

They drove through towering sugarcane that was as tall as a bus, making the thugs visibly uneasy. Ghost enjoyed watching them squirm.

He glanced sideways at the arms dealer sitting next to him. *Your days as a free man are numbered, you ruthless bastard.*

"I don't like this, Alek," Ramirez shouted, banging on the dividing window. In the rearview mirror, Ghost could see sweat patches spreading under Ramirez's arms. "Something's off."

Markov frowned. It was clear he didn't like it either, and while they might have Becca as insurance, Ghost was still calling the shots. He was the only one who knew where the merchandise was.

Besides, they'd taken his phone, so he couldn't warn Pat about Becca being held hostage.

This was happening whether he liked it or not.

He had to stop Markov before he gave Carlos the order to kill her. The gunrunner would do it the moment things went sideways. Failure wasn't an option. Becca's life was on the line.

Gritting his teeth, Ghost pulled the truck to a stop in front of the barn.

Markov and Ramirez, flanked by the two armed thugs, got out of the pickup. Ghost took his time, letting their nerves stew even more.

"Where are the buyers?" Ramirez snapped, swatting at a fly.

"They'll be here soon," Ghost replied.

While they waited, he walked to the barn door, pulled back a loose board on a side panel, and entered the ten-digit code that Miguel had given him when the merchandise had been stored. The code changed with every delivery.

One of the thugs snorted as the double doors swung open, released by a spring mechanism.

Ghost pushed them wide, and Markov marched inside. His face broke into a smile when he saw twenty crates stacked neatly in the center of the barn.

"Check it," he ordered the thugs, who rushed to inspect the goods.

"It's all here," one of them confirmed after opening several crates.

He had barely finished speaking when a low rumble echoed from the approach road. They stepped outside to investigate but could only see a dust cloud in the distance.

"That's them now," Ghost said. "Right on time."

They stood still as the dust cloud got closer, and soon they could make out a dark rectangular shape. As it neared, the shape became an eighteen-wheeler.

"What the hell are they bringing that for?" Markov asked with disdain. "You can see them coming from a mile away."

Ghost knew why: they had a small army hidden inside, along with crates of papaya, avocados, rice, or whatever other produce they were using to hide the weapons.

"Things work a little differently here," he said. European and Middle Eastern buyers preferred to keep things low-key, but out here, there was safety in numbers. That's why they needed the new weapons—more firepower meant more respect.

Ramirez was shifting uneasily again, sweat soaking through his shirt. Markov, outwardly calm, betrayed his tension through his clenched jaw. The two thugs took up defensive positions, legs apart, knees slightly bent, weapons trained on the approaching truck.

"Don't make any sudden moves," Ghost warned. "They can be a little jumpy."

He would know. He'd been dealing with the cartels for years and understood how they operated. His pulse didn't even quicken as the truck came to a stop and twelve heavily armed men jumped out, carrying assault rifles and submachine guns, all aimed at them.

"Put down your weapons," Ghost told the thugs. It was pointless to fight—they were outgunned.

The man in charge of the cartel delegation nodded. "Do what he says."

The leader was about forty, with piercing black eyes and a stocky build. Despite the heat, he wore a starched white shirt, open at the neck, and black trousers, giving off a flamenco-style vibe. Ghost had to admit, he looked sharp. It was clear from the way the others deferred to him that he was calling the shots.

Markov gestured to his men, and they reluctantly lowered their guns.

"Kick them over," barked the cartel leader.

As the thugs kicked their weapons away, Markov stepped forward, holding out his hand with a congenial smile.

"Alek Markov," he said, his voice impressively calm. Dom knew the man had ice in his veins. Markov had been conducting deals like this for years, always managing to stay cool in dangerous situations. He had the hard-man stare down to an art. With a nod, he added, "Pleasure doing business with you."

"Federico," said the man in charge.

They shook hands, and some of the tension in the air lifted.

Markov locked eyes with Federico. "I expect you'll want to inspect the merchandise."

CHAPTER 25

The Colombian nodded, and they went inside the barn. Two of Federico's men followed, while two positioned themselves at the barn entrance, two stayed outside, and four remained by the truck.

Ghost stood to the side and let Markov take charge. It was his merchandise, after all. Once the money changed hands, that's when the real action would begin.

He hugged the rough wooden walls, resisting the urge to glance up at the loft where the Blackthorn Security operatives were hiding. It was a good vantage point, allowing them to fire down if necessary. Like a castle, the loft was easy to defend if anyone tried climbing up the ladder to attack.

"You don't mind if we inspect the merchandise?" Federico's question was more of a statement than a request.

Markov spread his hands. "By all means."

The two mercenaries left his side and began inspecting the crates. They opened the top one and pulled out an AK-47 assault rifle, checking it over, disassembling and reassembling it before nodding at their boss. "Seems legit."

"Check the others," Federico barked.

They moved through the crates, which contained machine guns, RPGs, and other lethal equipment. All twenty crates were accounted for. Finally, Federico nodded and gestured to one of the men at the barn door. The man disappeared outside to the truck, returning with a sleek tablet. He powered it on and handed it to his boss.

"One hundred and fifty million dollars, as agreed."

Markov nodded, his eyes gleaming as he watched the cartel buyer orchestrate the payment.

Almost time.

His gaze drifted up to the rafters, but there was no sound, no movement. He knew the Blackthorn operatives were up there, invisible to those below. No one had thought to check the loft.

From above, a hidden camera was rolling, capturing the scene below. The men waiting in the jungle were prepared for a signal from inside before advancing. Their job was to take out the armed men by the truck and those guarding the barn perimeter.

The Blackthorn operatives in the loft would fire down, eliminating the interior guards, leaving Markov and Federico with no choice but to surrender.

That was Plan A.

But in true Marine fashion, Ghost had planned for every possible scenario. He knew from experience that things rarely went as planned.

Plan B involved a firefight—the most likely outcome. The guards would retaliate, people would get shot, and Markov and Federico would be captured in the chaos, if they were still breathing.

Plans C, D, and E covered contingencies in case Markov or Federico escaped into the jungle or the sugarcane fields, or if they took hostages. Other plans accounted for the possibility of losing any Blackthorn operatives or the key players themselves.

Federico handed Markov the tablet. "Transaction complete."

Let's go!

It was time.

Ghost, who was unarmed, backed into a corner where a rusty, unused tractor stood gathering dust. Taped to the underside was a handgun he'd need when the bullets started flying.

The floorboards above him creaked, and a loud voice rang out. "Put down your weapons. You're under arrest!"

Immediately, the two armed men at the door aimed high and opened fire, bullets slamming into the underside of the loft and ricocheting off the metal platform where the operatives lay. Pat, Blade, and Cole fired back, focusing on the guards, not Markov or Federico.

Ghost threw himself behind the tractor and slid beneath it, tearing the gun free from its hiding spot. He checked the chamber. Loaded.

He rolled onto his stomach and fired at Federico, but the Colombian was already being hustled out by two of his men. One fired behind them into the barn, while the other created cover outside. They weren't amateurs.

An all-out firefight erupted. Bullets flew from the edge of the jungle, and the cartel's militia fired back from behind the truck.

There was a yell as Ramirez took a hit to the shoulder, followed by another to the gut. The shots came from Federico's men, as far as Ghost could tell. Ramirez dropped to the ground, clutching his stomach, blood pooling around him. Ghost thought about pulling him to safety but figured with a gut wound like that, it probably wouldn't matter.

Markov sprinted for the exit, narrowly avoiding a hail of

bullets from above, and took off across the clearing into the sugarcane. Somehow, he avoided getting hit.

"Cover me!" Ghost shouted, running after him.

Pat, Blade, and Cole immediately provided cover fire, sliding down the ladder from the loft like firemen on a pole. Their rapid fire created a gap, allowing Ghost to sprint to the cane field.

The cartel's small army was now trapped, shooting wildly in all directions as they fended off incoming fire from the Colombian military advancing through the jungle, as well as the two FBI agents and the Blackthorn operatives in the barn.

Ghost left them to it and raced after Markov.

Shit.

He had to catch him before he gave Carlos the kill order.

There was no doubt in Ghost's mind that Carlos would execute Becca. He just hoped that in the chaos, Markov hadn't managed to send the message yet.

Ghost scanned the path splitting the sugarcane field but couldn't spot the arms dealer. Markov must've veered off into the dense cane, where he could stay hidden but would also be slowed down.

Ghost looked for broken stems or disturbed plants—anything that might show where Markov had entered the field. He couldn't hear him running, thanks to the gunfire behind him.

Time's running out.

Desperation sharpening his focus, Ghost retraced his steps and peered into the thick cane.

There!

Several stalks had recently been broken, sap still oozing. The ground beneath was flattened and disturbed. Markov had gone in there.

Ghost plunged into the field, grateful for his ankle-high army boots. The bastard he was chasing was wearing loafers, which would make running through this mess a nightmare. It wasn't hard to follow the trail as Markov bulldozed his way through the cane, falling every few yards.

"Markov!" Ghost shouted.

The arms dealer turned, twisting his body to fire a shot in Ghost's direction.

Ghost ducked as the bullet embedded itself in the cane. Close, but he'd been expecting it. He didn't fire back. He needed Markov alive.

The bastard would pay for what he'd done to Becca, rotting in a Colombian prison for the rest of his miserable life. Death was too easy.

Markov pushed on. Ghost followed.

He was gaining on him, but every few seconds, Markov would turn and fire, forcing Ghost to dive for cover. His aim was terrible, hampered by the dense cane and the uneven terrain.

"It's over, Markov!" Ghost's voice echoed through the field. "There's nowhere to run!"

Markov stopped, realizing he was cornered.

Slowly, he turned to face his pursuer.

For a moment, Ghost thought he was surrendering, but he had underestimated the slimy bastard. Markov held up his phone. "Back off, or she dies."

Ghost could tell by his voice he wasn't bluffing.

He froze, but kept his gun leveled at Markov's head.

One shot. That's all it would take. He could end this right now, blow the bastard's brains out and be done with it.

"I said, stand down." Markov's finger hovered over the send button.

Ghost slowly lowered his arm.

Fuck.

He couldn't risk it. Not with Becca's life on the line.

"Toss the gun," Markov ordered.

Ghost hesitated, then threw the gun into the cane. He wasn't about to hand it over for Markov to use as backup.

"Stay there," the arms dealer cautioned. "One move, and Carlos knows what to do."

Ghost glared but didn't move.

Markov began inching away, eyes on his phone. He pushed a button, then slipped the phone into his jacket pocket.

No fucking way.

Had he just sent the kill order?

Over my dead body.

Markov wasn't going to murder Becca *and* vanish into the ether.

Ghost dove into the cane, tearing it apart until he found his gun.

Markov zigzagged madly through the stalks, trying to make himself harder to hit. Ghost could only catch glimpses of his dark jacket, but that didn't matter. He stood, gun gripped in both hands. He stilled his breathing, focused, and anticipated where Markov would dodge next.

A low exhale—then he squeezed the trigger.

The shot echoed through the field. Ghost heard a sharp cry and saw Markov spin from the impact.

Gotcha.

Ghost sprinted forward. He had to get that phone and call Carlos off.

When he reached Markov, the arms dealer was on his knees, clutching his bloody shoulder.

"Give me the phone," Ghost growled, gun aimed at Markov's head.

"It's too late," Markov hissed, tossing the phone at him.

Fuck, no!

Ghost picked it up and stared at the message on the screen.

His chest constricted.

Kill the girl.

It had been sent.

CHAPTER 26

"You bastard!"

Ghost turned back to Markov, only to find the snake had slithered off again into the cane field.

Raising his weapon, he fired, but the hollow click told him the cartridge was empty.

Shit.

He tossed the gun away in disgust.

He was about to go after the arms dealer when the phone in his hand beeped. Glancing down, Ghost saw a red exclamation mark next to the sent message.

Only one bar.

No reception. They were in a dead zone.

He felt weak with relief.

Thank you, God.

He knew the message would send as soon as it found a signal, but at least this bought him some time.

He was itching to go after Markov and finish the job. He wanted to beat him senseless and leave his rotting corpse to be eaten by rats in this very field.

But he had precious little time to get to Becca.

There was still a chance he could outrun the text message.

Dropping the phone where he stood, Ghost turned and raced back to the clearing.

"You get him?" Pat strode out of the barn, rifle slung over his shoulder. The clearing looked like the aftermath of a warzone. The Colombian military was rounding up cartel members who weren't bleeding out on the ground, cuffing their wrists and loading them into the back of their own truck.

Ghost shook his head. "Bastard got away, but I hit him in the shoulder. He won't be hard to track."

Pat frowned. "It's not like you to miss. What's up?"

Ghost ran a hand through his messy hair. "Markov gave the kill order on Becca. They were using her as leverage."

Pat's face darkened. "Shit, I didn't know."

"There wasn't time to tell you. I've got to get back to the hacienda."

In the background, Blade was on the sat phone, calling for an evac helo. Cole was talking with two serious-looking Americans—probably the FBI guys.

"You want the helo?" Pat asked.

"Nah, I'll take the Cessna. It's faster." The chopper would take too long, and Ghost didn't have that kind of time.

Pat slapped him on the back. "Call if you need backup."

Ghost nodded. "Will do."

He jumped into the pickup and floored it down the dirt road to the waiting aircraft. His mind raced. Markov was injured, and he'd have to walk a few miles, while Ghost had the advantage of wheels. Plus, the plane was still there—he hadn't seen it take off.

But he'd forgotten about the guard they'd left behind.

"What's going on?" the thug demanded as Ghost leaped from the pickup. "I heard gunfire. Where's the boss?"

Gunfire? That was an understatement—they'd been in a firefight for over twenty minutes. *Coward.*

Without hesitation, Ghost smashed his fist into the guy's face, dropping him instantly. He snagged the Glock that fell beside him. There wasn't time to explain. Besides, the guy owed him for the gut punch earlier.

The pilot flinched at the violence, but Ghost leveled the Glock at him. "Get this thing in the air. We're leaving."

The pilot swallowed his objections and started the engine. Ghost climbed into the cockpit, strapped in, and within moments, they were taxiing down the narrow road, ready for takeoff.

Ghost knew Pat had the situation locked down. They had the whole transaction on video, which meant they now had everything they needed to take down Markov and Federico.

It was just a matter of time. There was nowhere left for Markov to hide. He'd never operate in this area again, and if he set foot in the U.S., he'd be arrested for attempted murder, money laundering, arms dealing, and a laundry list of other felonies.

He was done.

As they lifted off into the night sky, Ghost made a vow—he'd hunt Markov down, even if it was the last thing he ever did. But first, he had to get to Becca.

"Head north," he told the stunned pilot. "We're going to Panama."

CHAPTER 27

Please let her still be alive.

They flew north, up the west coast toward Panama and the Villa del Mar hacienda. The Pacific Ocean below shimmered like an oil slick—dark and foreboding.

As they neared the hacienda, Ghost turned his attention to the next problem. *Where the hell were they going to put her down?*

"We're out of gas," the pilot croaked, his voice strained. Right on cue, the little Cessna sputtered and began losing altitude. "We have to land."

Markov's sprawling estate, dimly lit by outdoor lamps and the underwater pool light—glowing like a blue homing beacon—came into view.

"Take her down," Ghost ordered.

"Where?"

Ghost could hear the panic in the pilot's voice. The plane was dropping fast.

"There!" He pointed to the approach road that stretched from the neighboring village to the estate. It was a few miles long, straight, and though not smooth, it was better than the dirt track they'd landed on at Miguel's farm. But without landing lights, it was hidden in the darkness.

The pilot squinted through the windshield. "I can't see it."

Ghost could only make it out because he knew it was there.

"I'll guide you." He leaned forward, eyes locked on the ground, searching for the break in the vegetation that marked the strip of tarmac. He made small corrections as they descended, until the pilot was lined up with the road. Seeing no headlights, they knew the path was clear.

They dropped lower, decreasing speed and altitude until they were just above the ground. The plane hovered, almost suspended in the air, before the wheels screeched as they made contact with the tarmac.

Ghost exhaled softly.

They'd made it.

The plane taxied a few thousand feet before coming to a halt.

"Gracias a Dios," the pilot breathed, collapsing in his seat.

"Yeah, that," Ghost muttered. "Thanks for the ride." He jumped down from the cockpit onto the road.

"Hey, wait! How am I gonna get back?" the pilot called after him, but Ghost was already sprinting toward the hacienda.

He stopped at the wrought-iron gates, scanning for the security guards he knew were there. Two men, armed and under strict orders not to let anyone in. A camera was also positioned above the gate to capture any arrivals.

Ghost didn't have time to argue with the guards or risk alerting Carlos by starting a shootout. He bypassed the gate and headed toward the fence that surrounded the property.

It wasn't electrified, though it did have spikes at the top. Ghost ripped his shirt in two, wrapping the fabric around his hands for protection. Beyond the fence lay thick, impenetrable jungle vegetation. It wasn't patrolled because it was too dense to navigate, but there were sensors hidden in the undergrowth that would detect movement.

Luckily, he knew where they were.

Like any good Marine, he'd taken a walk one evening and deliberately set them off, noting their locations, response times, and generally giving Carlos a headache. It had been a fun exercise then, but now, that prep work was about to pay off.

Ghost zigzagged through the undergrowth, crouched low, the gun he'd taken from the tractor ready at his side.

Ten minutes in, he found the path leading to his cabin.

Crouching low, he sprinted the rest of the way, keeping an eye out for patrols. He slipped inside the cabin and went straight to the wooden cabinet in the living room. From the bottom drawer, he retrieved the emergency stash of cash he'd taped to the back.

They'd need it if they were going to lay low for a while —at least until they could rendezvous with Pat and his team.

After grabbing a fresh T-shirt and pulling it on, he slipped back into the bush behind the cabin. By now, he knew the route to the pool terrace like the back of his hand. It didn't take him long to reach it.

There was a guard sitting on a deck chair, taking a smoke break, his rifle casually slung over his shoulder.

When the boss is away...

They weren't expecting trouble.

Ghost snorted quietly to himself. *Well, trouble had just arrived.*

He maneuvered until he was directly behind the man, creeping forward inch by inch. After a quick glance around to ensure they were alone, he made his move.

In less than a minute, the guard was unconscious, his

cigarette still smoldering beside him—and Ghost had appropriated his rifle.

He checked it over and grunted in approval; it was fully loaded.

Grabbing the guard's ankles, Ghost dragged him into the undergrowth, covering the body with some branches and leaves. Then he stomped out the cigarette.

Moving as silently as a panther, he crept toward the house. The front entrance was out of the question, so he went to the patio door leading to Becca's apartment. The bedroom window was open. He pulled it wide and climbed through.

Step one complete. He was in the house.

Now, where were they keeping her?

From the photo, it looked like she was being held in a storeroom. Based on his earlier recon of the property, he figured it had to be near the pool equipment storage or some kind of pantry attached to the kitchen. There weren't many other places she could be.

Tucking the Glock into the back of his pants, rifle in hand, he stalked down the corridor, ignoring the camera that would capture his image. If they saw him unarmed, they might assume he'd just returned unexpectedly. He was a familiar face here by now. But one look at the AK in his hands, and they'd know he meant business.

Moving quickly, he headed toward the storage units. The house was eerily quiet. Where was everyone? No one came to stop him, so he assumed that with Markov in Colombia, security was either relaxed or nonexistent.

He took a right down the hall, passing two unlocked doors filled with gardening equipment and pool supplies. The third door was locked.

He knocked but got no response. If Becca was inside, she couldn't answer.

His body tensed.

Please don't let him be too late.

Without any lock-picking tools, he went for plan B: kicking the door down. It took a few hard kicks and several shoulder slams, but eventually, the door splintered and gave way.

"Becca!"

Ghost rushed to where she sat tied to a chair. Her head hung forward, and for a terrifying moment, he feared the worst. His heart pounded as he checked her pulse.

Thank God. She was still alive.

"You!" came a voice behind him.

Carlos.

Slowly, Ghost turned to face Becca's captor.

"What are you doing here?" Carlos barked, eyes narrowing as they landed on the rifle in Ghost's hands.

"What does it look like?" he growled.

Carlos drew his weapon, but Ghost launched himself at him before he could fire. Gunshots would alert the rest of the guards, and he needed to get Becca out alive.

Carlos pulled out a hunting knife, and the two men squared off. Ghost removed the magazine from his rifle and tossed it aside. He was going to enjoy this.

Carlos snarled, slashing at him, but Ghost sidestepped easily.

Nice try, asshole.

Ghost punched him in the stomach, dodging the knife again as Carlos grunted but stood his ground. The guy was sturdier than he looked. He came at Ghost again, eyes blazing, the knife glinting in the dim light.

"I'll kill you," Carlos sneered.

"Not if I kill you first," Ghost muttered, dodging another strike and landing a solid right hook to Carlos's head.

Carlos staggered but recovered, advancing again.

Becca moaned softly, drawing his attention for a split second—enough time for Carlos to slash him across the upper arm.

He grunted in pain but didn't back down.

You get one. That's it.

Enough was enough.

As much as Ghost would have enjoyed round two, Becca needed him, and they had to get out of here. At any moment, the Panamanian police could show up.

He kicked the knife out of Carlos's hand, grinning at the look of shock on the henchman's face. The blade flew across the room, sliding under some boxes.

Ghost closed in, pummeling Carlos in the face, breaking his nose and splitting his lip. "How's that feel, you brute?"

He kept hitting him until Carlos stumbled backward and crumpled to the floor. Ghost didn't stop until he was sure the guy wasn't getting up again.

Becca moaned, and Ghost straightened, wiping his bloody knuckles on his pants. He grabbed the knife and cut through Becca's bindings, catching her as she slumped forward into his arms. He ripped the tape off her mouth and pressed a gentle kiss to her lips. Her eyelids fluttered but didn't open.

"I've got you," he murmured, his heart aching at the sight of her bruised, swollen face. *Carlos deserved everything he got.*

Ghost picked her up, kicking Carlos in the ribs as he carried her out.

He made his way through the kitchen and out the back toward the garages. Shifting Becca's weight over his shoulder, he grimaced as his injured left arm took the strain, but he needed his right free for the rifle. There were still guards on patrol and if they hadn't heard the ruckus inside, they'd soon find Carlos's body and the place would be shut down.

"Who are you?"

Ghost spun around, weapon poised. One of Carlos's men was pointing a rifle at him.

"I've got to get her to a doctor," he said, taking a chance and lowering the weapon. The man wouldn't know he was rescuing her. "I work for Markov, this is his personal assistant."

The man hesitated, his gaze wandering over Becca. From where he was standing, he couldn't see her face.

"She's hurt, there's been an accident," Dom insisted. "The boss wouldn't want anything to happen to her while he's away."

The man nodded and pressed a remote, which raised the garage door. Dom ducked inside and laid Becca on the back seat of the SUV. He'd no more than closed the door before he heard shouting outside.

"Stop him!" came the cry in Spanish.

Shit.

They'd found Carlos's body!

Ghost jumped into the driver's seat and started the engine. Luckily, the keys were always kept in the ignition in case of emergencies. Markov's orders. He never knew when he'd have to make a quick exit.

The garage door began to lower, but Ghost revved the SUV and took off, accelerating through it. The bottom half went flying.

The two guards jumped back as he roared past them down the driveway. The vegetation on either side flew by in a green blur. There was some incoming fire at the gate as the guards tried half-heartedly to stop him, but he blasted through with a crunch of twisted metal.

Becca was still unconscious on the back seat. This wasn't good, she was in a bad way.

He pushed the SUV as hard as it would go, past the light aircraft that had been abandoned by the side of the road, skidding around corners and smoking on the worn tarmac until he reached the nearest village.

It was in darkness, having shut down for the night. He decreased his speed and cruised until he came across a tiny cantina, which was little more than a lit window in a wall.

Good enough.

He pulled over, giving the young couple making out in front a fright.

"Which way to the nearest doctor?" he asked, in Spanish.

When they just stared at him, he reiterated, "Doctor? Clinic? Hospital?"

"Ah, si," said the young man and rattled off an address.

Ghost shook his head and pointed down the road. "Dónde?" Where?

The girl gave him directions. He nodded his thanks.

"The clinic will be shut," she shouted after him, "but the doctor lives in the apartment above."

Ghost put his foot down, leaving skid marks behind him.

CHAPTER 28

El Centro Médico, read the sign above the glass-fronted brick building.

Finally.

Ghost pulled over and surveyed it. As the girl had said, it was dark. Hiding the rifle under the seat, he got out of the car and banged on the door.

No answer.

He craned his neck to look up at the apartment above. No lights were on. He turned back to the front door. There was no emergency after-hours number listed, but a side panel with buzzers—presumably for the apartments upstairs—caught his eye.

He rang them all. Eventually, a groggy female voice answered.

"Doctor?" Ghost asked. "It's an emergency."

"Number 3," the voice said, then hung up.

Ghost pressed the button for number 3 and kept his finger on the buzzer until someone answered.

"¿Sí?" came an annoyed voice.

Ghost repeated his request for a doctor and added that he'd pay in dollars.

There was a pause, then the voice said, "I'm coming."

The clinic lights flickered on, and a few moments later, a disheveled, middle-aged man wearing pajamas pulled back the blind. He studied Ghost, then pursed his lips as if debating whether to let him in or not. It didn't take a genius to figure out what kind of man he was.

Ghost shifted his hand toward the Glock behind his back, ready to use it if necessary. Luckily, it wasn't. The doctor unlocked the door.

"You're hurt?" His eyes fixed on Ghost's knife wound.

"Not me." Ghost pointed to the car. "Her."

The doctor's eyebrows raised, and he waited as Ghost extracted Becca from the back seat and carried her into the clinic.

"Come."

The doctor led them through a door behind the reception desk into a small consulting room that smelled faintly of antiseptic. He switched on a fluorescent overhead light and pulled back a plastic curtain. Behind it was a metal bed with a pillow and a strip of paper toweling over it.

"Put her there."

Ghost gently lowered Becca onto the bed. She groaned but didn't wake up.

The doctor's eyes widened as he took in the bruises on her face and arms, the cracked lip, the swelling on her temple. "What happened?"

Wasn't it obvious? "Someone beat her up," Ghost replied.

"You from the hacienda?" The doctor bent down to examine Becca's head wound.

When Ghost didn't answer immediately, the doctor glanced up. "I don't want any trouble."

Ghost spread his hands. "I'm not here to cause trouble. Can you help her?"

The doctor went back to inspecting Becca, gently feeling along her shoulder blade. She winced, and he nodded. "She's got a concussion and a broken collarbone, but aside from that, I think she'll be okay. The bruises on her face will heal."

Ghost exhaled.

Thank God.

"So, she's going to be okay?"

"I think so. She needs a head scan, but I'll do what I can for now."

"Thanks, Doc."

Ghost watched as the doctor cleaned and treated Becca's head wound, then moved on to her split lip, gently wiping away the blood and disinfecting the cut. "I need to reset her collarbone. It's best to do it now while she's still unconscious."

Ghost nodded. "Do what you have to."

The doctor took Becca's arm and gently pulled it outward, rotating it externally. There was a loud pop as the bone relocated back into place.

Becca murmured but didn't wake.

"You sure she's going to be okay?" Ghost asked, worried. That was a painful procedure, yet she barely reacted.

"As sure as I can be without a brain scan," the doctor replied. "You need to get her to a hospital as soon as she can be moved. The nearest one is twelve miles from here, east of the city."

Ghost nodded. Whatever it took to make sure she was okay. In the background, sirens screamed down the road toward the hacienda.

The doctor looked up. "Are those for you?"

"Not us. We just worked there. They're after the bad guys."

The doctor gave him a curt nod and continued his work.

After tending to Becca, he cleaned and stitched Ghost's knife wound. "You get this saving her?"

Ghost nodded. "You should see the other guy."

The doctor chuckled. It was the first time he'd relaxed since they walked in.

"Thanks for patching us up," Ghost said as the doctor finished tying a bandage around his upper arm. He handed him a wad of U.S. dollars. "Will a hundred cover it?"

The doctor nodded and pocketed the money. "You can't move her yet. She needs rest."

"We've got to get out of here," Ghost said, not wanting to go into too much detail. It wasn't that he didn't trust the doctor, but he knew that if push came to shove, the man would do what was necessary to protect himself and his family.

"You can go, but she has to stay," the doctor insisted.

Ghost could have easily taken Becca and walked out, but he knew the doctor was right. Rest was the best thing for her.

"I'll be back in a few hours." He needed to ditch the SUV before the authorities traced it here or someone spotted it outside the clinic.

The doctor nodded. "Sí, go ahead. She'll be fine. I will check on her."

Ghost shook his hand. "Thanks. Turn off the lights in reception so no one knows you're here." He didn't mention that people would be looking for him.

"Okay."

The doctor walked him to the door and let him out into the dark street. A moment later, he saw the clinic lights go out and heard the bolt slide into place behind the door.

He heaved a sigh of relief. Becca was safe, for now.

. . .

Ghost drove the SUV around the corner, out of sight from the main road. It was the same road that led to the hacienda, hence the sudden rush of police vehicles. He made it just in time before two more police cars sped past, lights flashing.

They'd be disappointed. There was nothing left to find except a bunch of hired thugs. Most of them would probably scatter the moment they heard the sirens. He doubted the guards at the gate would even try to stop the police.

Without Markov there to give orders, they'd melt into the jungle or slip down to the beach. No one wanted to get arrested—not for a boss who didn't even know their names.

He continued driving until the road steepened and turned into a dirt track. Pulling over under some trees, he rummaged in the glove box and found what he was looking for—a map.

Bingo. Thanks, Carlos.

He switched on the overhead light and studied it.

As expected, there was a small body of water a couple of miles ahead. One thing you could always find in a tropical country was a lake.

He shifted the SUV into four-wheel drive and veered off the dirt road onto a barely visible trail. After ten minutes of bumping uphill, the trail ended, and he found himself facing the dark, glassy surface of a lake.

He grabbed the map, the rifle, and a spare cartridge from the glove compartment, then drove the SUV as close to the water's edge as he dared. The lake looked deep and uninviting—the perfect burial site for the SUV.

Leaving the car in neutral, he released the brake and pushed it into the water. It gained momentum thanks to the slight slope, and soon it was gone. A few loud glugs and the black vehicle disappeared into the depths.

Good luck finding that one.

Ghost turned and began hiking back to the main road.

The night air was cool against his skin, although technically, it was almost morning. The sky was starting to glow faintly in the east, signaling daybreak was about an hour away.

He picked up the pace, settling into a gentle jog. It reminded him of rucking through Afghanistan or Iran during ops, hours spent moving out of enemy territory. This wasn't much different—he had to make it back to the clinic before the sun fully rose.

By the time he reached the village, dawn had broken. The streets were light enough that anyone passing by would notice him, but so far, the village seemed still asleep. Thankfully, the locals weren't early risers.

He rang the buzzer, and the doctor's voice crackled through the speaker. "Coming."

A few moments later, Ghost stood in the clinic reception while the doctor eyed the rifle warily.

"It's just for protection." He ejected the magazine and checked the chamber before setting the gun down, well out of reach.

He must've looked like hell. The shirt he'd thrown on a few hours ago was now covered in dust, dried sweat, and blood seeping through his bandage. The doctor, now dressed and no longer in pajamas, gave him a quick once-over.

"How is she?" Ghost asked.

"Sleeping," the doctor replied with a nod, as if confirming it was the right thing. Ghost agreed.

"Good."

An awkward pause followed.

"Mind if I use your bathroom to freshen up?"

"Sí." He pointed down a sterile corridor. "There's one for the patients. You can use that." His eyes lingered on Ghost's dirty, blood-stained shirt. "I'll find you some clean clothes. They might be a little small, but I'll see what I have."

"Appreciate it."

In the small bathroom, Ghost scrubbed every inch of his body, even washing his hair. The tiny space didn't allow much room, but it felt good to get clean. Water pooled on the floor, so he used paper towels to dry himself and tidied the bathroom until it was spotless.

God, it felt good to be clean.

His body ached from exhaustion, and his bicep was sore around the wound. The doc had slathered it with antibiotic ointment, so he hoped it would heal without further trouble.

When he emerged, he saw a pile of clothes on one of the waiting room chairs. The doctor, a tall man—probably about five-ten or five-eleven—was much slimmer than Ghost. The sweatpants fit, but were tight across his thighs, and the T-shirt clung to his chest and biceps, pressing against his wound. Ghost ripped the sleeve at the back to loosen it. That was better. It wasn't perfect, but it would do.

He checked on Becca. She lay motionless on the steel table, a blanket draped over her. She seemed to be resting peacefully.

Ghost gently touched her pale face. "You're okay now," he whispered.

A wave of exhaustion swept over him, and he glanced around for somewhere to sit. The doc had a comfortable-looking leather chair tucked under his desk. He pulled it out, stretched his legs, and sat down. Now that the adrenaline had worn off, his body was ready to shut down. As the village began to stir, Ghost drifted off into a deep sleep.

CHAPTER 29

"Where am I?"

Becca opened her eyes and saw the sterile white walls of a hospital ward. She was hooked up to a machine that beeped intermittently, while a nurse hovered around her bed, checking her vitals.

"Welcome back," the nurse smiled at her. "You've been out for quite a while."

Becca tried to sit up, but her arms felt weak, and a persistent ache throbbed in her shoulder. With a sigh of defeat, she flopped back down.

"Come on, let's get you comfortable."

The nurse propped her up with extra pillows. She had a kind face and an American accent. "You're at the Hospital Nacional. You've had a bad concussion and a broken collarbone, but you're on the mend now."

Okay, that was good news. It wasn't serious.

Her memory was still foggy, but she hadn't forgotten Carlos laying into her before she'd passed out.

She glanced around. The ward was empty except for her.

The other two beds were unoccupied. How had she gotten here?

"There's someone outside waiting to see you," the nurse said.

Oh no. *Alek.*

He must've found her and wanted to take her home. She remembered how he'd handed her over to Carlos without a flicker of emotion when he thought she'd betrayed him.

A cold shiver ran down her spine. Carlos had made her talk—made her give up Dom. She'd told him everything.

Her eyes filled with tears. If she'd betrayed anyone, it was Dom.

"Who is it?" she asked hesitantly. "I'm not sure I'm up to seeing anyone."

The nurse frowned. "Well, he's anxious to see you. He's the one who brought you in yesterday. He's been so worried, poor thing. He must really care about you."

"Worried?" No way—it couldn't be her father.

"I wish I had a good-looking man like that worried about me." The nurse winked.

Good-looking? Becca's breath caught. Was it possible?

"Dom?"

"Yes, I think that's the name he gave the nurse at the front desk."

Becca's heart swelled with joy. He was alive! And better than that, he'd come back for her. She vaguely remembered his voice telling her she'd be okay, his strong arms carrying her, the gentle rocking of a car. She thought she'd dreamed it...

Had it actually happened? She broke into a smile, then winced as her lip and cheek stung.

The nurse grinned. "That's what I thought. I'll send him in, shall I?"

Becca nodded.

The nurse left the room, and immediately the door burst open, and Dom rushed in.

"You're awake, thank God."

He appeared more flustered than she'd ever seen him, but damn if he didn't look good.

She drank him in with her eyes. He cleaned up well. Gone were the combat gear and T-shirt. He was dressed in denim jeans that hugged his thighs and butt, and a black shirt, open at the neck, with the sleeves rolled up, showing off his tanned, toned forearms.

Her mouth went dry.

In those clothes, with that jaw and physique, he was irresistible.

"You had me so worried." He sat on the edge of the bed. "When you wouldn't wake up, I thought Carlos had done some permanent damage."

Carlos.

The memories came flooding back—and with them, the guilt.

"Oh, Dom, I'm so sorry. I told him about you, about who you were. I couldn't help it. They made me talk. They put my head in a bucket of water—I couldn't breathe. I tried not to tell them, but then he hit me over and over again. I just wanted it to stop."

Dom's mouth set in a grim line. Oh no, he was mad at her.

"I'm so sorry. I didn't mean to betray you."

"Shh... it's okay." He grasped her hand. "They showed me a photograph of what that bastard had done to you, hoping it'd scare me into cooperating, but I saw red. I knew then I'd come back and beat the crap out of Carlos."

"And did you?" she whispered, hoping he had. That lecherous brute deserved everything he got. She'd never forget the look of satisfaction on his face as he hit her.

He scoffed. "And then some."

She squeezed his hand. "Thank you for rescuing me. I don't know how you managed it, but I owe you my life."

"It's a long story," he said. "But I've got some friends here who helped me, and they're dying to meet you. Can I invite them in?"

Becca looked confused. "Friends? Who?"

Sensing her hesitation, Dom added, "They're good guys. Trust me, you're going to want to hear what they have to say."

She nodded and lay back as three men and a woman entered the room. They all stood around her bed. The men were big and bulky like Dom, clearly fellow soldiers, though dressed casually in jeans and shirts.

The woman stood out. She was pale and slender but toned, like a runner. She stood confidently, legs apart, arms folded, watching Becca with open curiosity. Her long strawberry-blond hair was tied back in a ponytail, and her delicate features seemed to get more striking the longer you looked at her.

"Hi," Becca said, suddenly nervous.

What could these people have to tell her that she didn't already know? Her father was a crook, a gunrunner, a murderer, and probably a psychopath, so nothing they said could shock her.

Dom made the introductions. "This is Pat. He's the one who orchestrated this whole undercover op and recruited me. Blade and Cole are part of his unit, and this is Thorn, who saved the man your father tried to have killed earlier this year."

Becca managed a small smile. She still didn't know why they were here, though.

Pat stood out as the leader, despite being at least ten, maybe even fifteen years older than the others. He had a powerful presence that demanded attention. Even though the other men were impressive, it was Pat who drew the eye.

He was a good-looking man, with short dark hair graying at the temples, broad shoulders, a rugged face that spoke of years of combat, and a steely, unsettling gaze that seemed to pierce right through you.

Dom sat back down on the edge of her bed, resting his hand on her leg under the covers. She liked feeling it there—it was reassuring, yet somehow disturbing and exciting all at once.

God, these pain meds must be messing with my head.

Even concussed and in a hospital bed, she was attracted to him.

"It's good to meet you, Becca," Pat said. "We wanted to let you know we apprehended your father."

Her eyes shot to Dom for confirmation.

He nodded. "The delivery didn't go as planned. The cartel arrived with a small army, and in the firefight that followed, Markov and the cartel negotiator escaped. I went after him, but when I saw he'd ordered Carlos to kill you, I let him go and raced back to the hacienda."

"Luckily, Markov was injured," Pat cut in. "So tracking him wasn't hard."

"Injured?"

"Yeah, I shot him." Dom cleared his throat.

Becca nodded sadly. It was inevitable. "But you let him get away because of me."

"Only temporarily," Blade said. "We had the evidence we needed to arrest him, so when he tried to board a plane to Argentina, we nabbed him."

Becca shook her head. "Argentina? I'm surprised he even has anywhere left to run."

"It's a good thing we caught him," Pat added. "The cartel paid for the shipment of weapons, and now they want their money back. They don't take kindly to being robbed. If we hadn't found him when we did, they would've hunted him down—and I can promise you, they wouldn't have been nearly as lenient as the Colombians."

Becca shivered. The way he said that made her blood run cold.

"Isn't he still at risk?" she asked, knowing the cartels could get to people even in prison. No one was truly safe. She'd lived here long enough to understand how they operated.

"Yes, but he'll give the money back," Blade replied. "He knows it's only a matter of time before they find him."

"And we don't want them coming after you either," Dom added.

"That won't bother Alek," Becca said weakly. "He doesn't care about me. That word's not even in his vocabulary."

Dom rubbed her leg gently. Pat noticed, his all-seeing gaze flickering between them.

The woman, Thorn, spoke for the first time. "Becca—Do you mind if I call you that?"

Becca shook her head. "I prefer it, anyway. I haven't been that person in a long time."

Thorn nodded. "I'm sorry to bring up bad memories, but the person your father had a hit out on, the person I was assigned to protect, was your ex-husband, Damian Clayton."

Becca gasped. "Damian?"

She stared at the woman for a long moment. "Alek tried to kill Damian for deserting him?"

"No, it wasn't because of that." The woman took a step closer to the bed. "They resolved those differences years ago. The reason Markov wanted to terminate Damian was because he'd developed an important upgrade to his cryptocurrency software that would decrypt his clients' illegal transactions on the dark web."

It took a minute for that to sink in. Alek's words came back to her.

He's the reason I had to leave America.

"So, Alek's illegal online transactions wouldn't remain anonymous? He'd be exposed."

"That's right." Thorn smiled. She really was very beautiful with that gorgeous hair and pale skin, the hint of a rosy blush in her cheeks. "The FBI managed to decipher the encrypted transactions and issued a warrant for his arrest."

"That's why he fled here."

Rose nodded. "He came to Central America because he had a stockpile of black-market arms and needed a buyer. He thought the cartels might be interested, and of course, they were."

Becca exhaled. It was a lot to take in. "I knew he was up to no good when I lived with him all those years ago," she confided. "But time makes you forget, and I never knew the extent of it. I'm glad Damian is okay."

There was an awkward silence.

"He *is* okay, isn't he?" She glanced between them, a sick feeling building in her stomach. What weren't they telling her?

"Yes, he's okay," said Thorn, her cheeks flushing. "In fact, he's here now, and he'd like to talk to you, if you're feeling up to it. I believe you guys have some unresolved issues."

Becca swayed, even though she was sitting down.

Some unresolved issues.

Yeah, you could say that. Like why the hell she'd walked out on him two days after they got married. Those kinda issues.

"Maybe now isn't such a good time." Dom frowned, concerned.

"No, it's fine," she croaked. She may as well get this over with. It had already been a crappy week. "It's just a shock, that's all. I haven't seen Damian in nearly a decade. Why does he want to talk to me now?"

"I'll let him explain," Thorn said.

"We'll leave you to talk." Pat nodded at her. "It was good to meet you, Becca. I'm sorry for all you went through, but it's over now."

"Thank you," she replied, resisting the urge to add "sir." He was just that kind of man.

Dom stood up and made to go.

"No, stay." She reached out to him.

He hesitated. "Are you sure?"

"Please."

Confronting Damian alone was more than she could bear. Dom's presence by her side gave her strength, and she was drawing on that right now. He made her feel like she could do anything. Confronting her demons was part of that.

He glanced at Thorn, who nodded, and sat down again.

Becca was confused. What did Thorn have to do with Damian? Sure, she'd been his bodyguard, but he'd survived the attack on his life. He must have done if he was here, ready to confront her. The private security contract was over.

It was then that she noticed the engagement ring on Thorn's finger. It was enormous, beautiful and sparkly, but now that she'd noticed it, she couldn't stop staring at it.

Surely not?

The others filed out of the hospital ward, and a second later, the door swung open, and in walked her ex-husband.

CHAPTER 30

"Hello, Rebecca," Damian said as he walked in.

Becca blinked, her breath catching in her throat.

Rebecca.

No one had called her that in years. The way the name rolled off his tongue, so casual, so unaffected—it threw her off. She hadn't expected Damian to sound so calm. She sure as hell didn't feel calm. The name alone sent a surge of guilt, anxiety, and... something else. Panic, maybe? It had been a long time since she'd let anyone stir those feelings in her, and here he was, doing it effortlessly.

She stared at him, waiting for the surge of emotion to hit her, but it didn't come—not in the way she'd expected.

Ten years ago, she'd walked out on him during their honeymoon and never looked back. She'd run away in the middle of the night, leaving nothing but a note—no explanations, no phone call, just silence. She hadn't even stayed long enough to hear his response. The guilt had gnawed at her for years.

He was looking at her now with a faint smile, but she

couldn't shake the thought of how much she had hurt him. It had been an awful thing to do, and she could only imagine what he'd gone through. He'd been in love with her, she knew that, but she'd been young and a mess, and she'd panicked. She hadn't known what to do with herself, let alone with someone who genuinely cared about her.

Her mouth went dry. "Damian," she whispered.

He looked good. Much better than she remembered. The husband she'd left behind had been tall, slim, and kind of nerdy-looking, with his slightly crooked glasses and tousled hair that always seemed one gust of wind away from chaos.

This man standing before her was... *different*.

Self-assured. Confident. His easy smile didn't carry any of the uncertainty she remembered, and those crinkly eyes, like he laughed more often now, were nothing like the intense, brooding stares he used to give her. What a change from the man she'd married.

Becca expected a flood of emotions, something more than guilt, but instead, there was an overwhelming sadness that things had ended the way they had. The fondness she'd once felt for him was like a distant echo, hollowed out by time and her own decisions.

Yet, there was still that guilt.

How could she ever make it right?

"I'm sorry for leaving the way I did," she blurted out, feeling the need to say something, *anything*, to break the silence. The apology felt raw, awkward, tumbling out before she could catch it. "I didn't want to hurt you."

The vulnerability in her voice made her wince. She was supposed to be stronger now, but in front of Damian, she felt like that same scared, confused girl from a decade ago.

He walked over to the bed. "That's why I'm here. I wanted to say that I'm sorry too." His voice was gentle, genuine. "I know your father pressured you into marrying me, and I'm sorry I took advantage of the situation."

She swallowed hard. "*You're* sorry? I'm the one that should be apologizing."

"He's a bad man, Becca. It's a good thing he's finally behind bars."

A surge of emotion brought tears to her eyes. Damian had forgiven her. That meant more to her than anything else.

"I know," she whispered, her voice barely audible. "I guess I was hoping he'd change, but of course, that never happens. I should have learned my lesson last time." If she had, things with Damian might have been different.

"People can change," Damian said softly. "I've grown a lot in the years since I stopped working for Alek. I'm a completely different person now."

She studied him—his relaxed demeanor, the tanned arms and face, his ready smile. The transformation was undeniable. The pale, intense young man she had known was gone, replaced by someone who seemed at peace with himself.

She studied his relaxed demeanor, the tanned arms and face, his ready smile, and recalled the pale, intense young man he'd been ten years ago. "I can see that."

She felt Dom stiffen beside her.

"Are you happy, Damian?"

He glanced at Thorn, and Becca didn't miss the tender look that passed between them. She'd been right! Those carats on the operative's finger had been given to her by Damian.

"Yeah, I'm happy."

"Good." She smiled at the two of them. "I'm glad."

Becca met Thorn's gaze and an understanding passed between them. No more words were necessary. Thorn had captured her ex-husband's heart, and Becca was okay with that. More than okay. Damian deserved to be happy, and judging by the look of him, this woman was good for him.

Suddenly, the guilt she'd been carrying around for the last decade lifted.

She exhaled. It felt wonderful to be free of it at last.

"I'm glad you came to see me."

"When Pat told me what had happened, I thought it would be a good opportunity to put things right," Damian said. "Ten years is a long time to hold a grudge."

Becca cringed. "I felt so guilty, abandoning you like that, but I didn't know what else to do. I couldn't carry on with that farce any longer."

"It's okay," Damian said. "I didn't understand at the time, but over the years I've had plenty of time to think about it, and I realized how young you were and how Markov manipulated you. It wasn't fair, and I should have stopped it."

"You were young too," Becca whispered. "He used both of us."

"That he did," Damian said softly. "Anyway, we can talk some more when you're feeling better. We'll be in Panama for a few days. I just wanted to clear the air and say I'm glad you're okay."

"Thanks, Damian," she said, as Thorn took his hand and they left the room.

CHAPTER 31

Ghost watched Becca's head fall back onto the pillow as she closed her eyes. She looked pale, the confrontation had clearly taken its toll on her.

"Shall I give you some time alone, to process everything?" He got to his feet. He didn't want to leave, but seeing her ex-husband after all these years had been a shock, and she might need some space to wrap her head around it all.

Ghost hadn't known what to expect when Pat had told him Damian was flying in to see Becca. The billionaire cryptocurrency developer and his fiancée, Thorn, had arrived earlier that morning, and Ghost had spent the better part of the day with them, mostly hanging out in the hospital canteen, drinking bad coffee, and talking about Alek Markov and how the man had destroyed so many lives.

Ghost had wanted to catch Markov himself, to be there when the bastard was taken down, but Becca had needed him more. So he let Blackthorn Security take that honor. Still, he'd make sure he was at the trial. He wanted to savor the moment when Markov was led away in chains.

Ghost hadn't expected to warm up to Damian, let alone *like* him, but the more they talked, the more he realized Damian was the type of guy he could easily be friends with.

Straightforward, honorable, motivated, and above all, willing to do the right thing, no matter the cost to himself or his business.

It had been a surprise to learn Damian had fought on the front lines in northern Syria. Ghost had seen action there himself, serving with the Marine Corps and later in the special forces. It turned out they had more in common than he had anticipated.

Which only made it worse seeing Becca's reaction to him.

How could she *not* regret leaving a guy like that? Not only was he good-looking and a great guy, but he was also a fucking billionaire.

And now he was engaged to someone else.

Becca had missed her chance.

"I'm sorry it didn't work out between you two," he murmured, ignoring the gnawing feeling in his gut. How could he compete with that?

Her eyelids flickered open. "Why would you say that?"

He shrugged, covering his inner turmoil. "I saw how he affected you. I know it can't be easy seeing him again. You obviously cared about him."

Becca gave him a small smile. "I did, and I still do. He's a good man."

Ghost felt his heart shatter, like an IED going off inside him.

Then, something unexpected happened. Becca took his hand.

He froze, his gaze locking with hers.

"I'm glad he came to see me," she said softly. "Because now I can let go of the guilt I've been carrying around for the last decade. I felt terrible leaving him the way I did. I don't think a day has gone by where I haven't regretted it. But now that he's found someone else and he's happy, I can finally move on."

Ghost stared at her, hardly daring to hope. "You really mean that?"

"Of course. I don't have any romantic feelings for Damian anymore. I haven't for a long time. I don't think I was ever really in love with him. Not the kind of love that's real... not like..." She trailed off, her eyes flickering away from his face.

"What?" he whispered, gripping her hand tighter.

"Nothing, it's silly," she muttered, biting her lip.

"Tell me, Becca," he urged, sitting back down on the bed. "What were you going to say?"

She hesitated, her eyes darting back to their entwined fingers. "I was going to say, nothing like what I feel for you."

Ghost's heart stopped. Had she really said that? He waited, his mind racing, barely able to process the words.

He broke into a broad grin. "It's not silly, Becca. Shall I tell you why?"

She looked up at him, her eyes wide.

"Because I feel the same way about you."

"You do?" she whispered.

"Yes, I do. The first time I saw you, I knew you weren't like any other woman I'd ever met. Then, when we... well, after that first night in your apartment, I knew there was something special between us, but I couldn't admit it to myself. I figured I'd be going my way and you'd be going yours, so there wasn't any point in thinking about it."

He paused, searching her face for any sign that he'd said the wrong thing. She squeezed his hand, silently urging him to continue.

"When I saw those pictures of what Carlos had done to

you... I've never felt rage like that in my life. I knew I had to get back to the hacienda and get you out of there."

"How did you get back?" she asked, her voice hitching. "I told Carlos about you. They knew who you were. I thought for sure they'd kill you in Colombia."

"They used the photos to blackmail me into cooperating. They took my phone, so I had no way to contact anyone. I had to go ahead with the mission, despite the risk to you."

She shivered. "Carlos told me my fate was in your hands. I didn't understand what he meant, but now I do. He was going to kill me if you didn't cooperate."

Ghost clenched his jaw, the memory of those photos making his blood boil all over again. "He was going to kill you no matter what," he said quietly. "But I wasn't going to let that happen. I hijacked a plane and flew back through the night to get to you before the authorities did."

Her eyes widened. "You hijacked a plane?"

He chuckled. "A small one, but yeah. I'd do it again if it meant saving you."

She stifled a sob, her eyes welling with tears. "No one's ever done anything like that for me before."

He wrapped his arms around her, pulling her close. She was bruised, fragile, and smelled faintly of antiseptic, but to him, she was the most beautiful woman in the world. "I'll be there for you whenever you need me. You don't have to be alone anymore."

She buried her face in his neck. "I can't tell you how much that means to me. I'm so tired of running."

"You don't have to run anymore. Becca... I know we haven't known each other long, but..."

He took a deep breath, feeling the weight of his own words pressing down on him.

Just say it.

"I've fallen in love with you."

Her eyes went wide. "You have?"

Shit, what if he'd misread the situation? But no, he didn't care. He had to say it. He'd kept enough secrets in his life. He wasn't keeping this one.

"I don't know when it happened, but it's the truth."

A slow smile spread across her lips. "I have a confession of my own."

His heart skipped a beat. "You do?"

"You had me the first time you kissed me on the deck of your cabin. The sun was setting, and I remember thinking, what kind of man is this? A dangerous mercenary? An honorable soldier? Then you kissed me, and I knew."

"Knew what?"

"That you're both. A delicious mixture."

He grinned. "Even the dangerous part?"

Her eyes sparkled. "Especially the dangerous part."

Heat curled in his stomach. It was crazy how she could affect him with just one look. "Why didn't you say anything?"

"I was playing hard to get."

He laughed, shaking his head.

"I guess it worked."

"Yeah, it did."

He leaned in and kissed her, gently at first, then deeper as the warmth between them grew. It felt so right, like they were finally where they were supposed to be.

"I must look a mess," she murmured, pulling back slightly. She ran a hand through her hair, but it didn't do much good.

"You're beautiful," he said, meaning every word. Not just on the outside, but inside too. Her strength, her spirit, her loyalty, everything about her made him fall harder every day.

"I'm so happy right now," she whispered, her voice soft with emotion. "I feel like my life might finally have a happy ending. Is that crazy?"

"It will," he promised, brushing a strand of hair behind her ear. "I swear it."

He kissed her again, his lips lingering on hers, savoring the moment. They were still wrapped up in each other when the nurse came in to discharge her.

EPILOGUE

Becca clutched Dom's hand as they waited for the boarding gate to appear. She was really doing it. She was going back to America with her brave, warm-hearted, gorgeous man. Her mercenary, her soldier, her savior.

The last few days had been blissful. Dom had been so gentle with her, and she'd hardly left his side. They'd swum in the hotel pool, made love—repeatedly—in their suite, and dined with the other members of Blackthorn Security.

Becca had gotten to know and like them all. Pat wasn't nearly as intimidating as he'd seemed at first, though he could still give you a look that made the hairs on your neck stand up. Most of the time, though, he was like a big teddy bear.

Blade was the hardest to get to know. He was reserved but radiated strength and discipline, and she could tell he was an excellent soldier. Every now and then, he'd make a wicked, off-beat joke that reminded her he had a sharp sense of humor. He was especially funny after a few beers. She hadn't had the chance to meet his wife, Lily, a brilliant computer analyst who was working on a top-secret project for the U.S. government.

Cole was super friendly. He and Thorn—whose real name was actually Rose—were very close and kept everyone in stitches with their banter.

Damian didn't seem to mind his fiancée's friendship with Cole. In fact, Damian and Cole seemed to be good friends too. Later, Becca learned that Cole's wife, Anna, was expecting their first child any moment now, and he was eager to get back. "She told me to hurry, said she can't hold on much longer," he'd confessed before they left the hotel. Becca could see he was nervous but also excited to be a dad.

"How are you feeling?" Dom asked. He was nervous too, having not been back to the States in a long time.

She felt her passport in her back pocket and a shiver of excitement ran down her spine. "I've never felt better," she told him, loving how his face lit up.

Pat had promised to help her find a job through his contacts in Washington. "With your skills, you'll be snapped up in no time," he'd assured her. "In fact, I know someone whose executive assistant just left, and they're struggling to find someone who can keep up. I'll put you forward for the role."

Becca still couldn't believe how welcoming everyone had been. A new start, a new career, and an exciting future with the man she loved. It didn't get better than that.

They boarded the flight and took their seats. As the plane took off, Dom took her hand. "I believe this is what they call flying off into the sunset."

"You're such a romantic," she teased, leaning over to kiss him. Her lip was almost healed now and didn't hurt as much. Their kiss lingered, and she felt a familiar warmth spread through her body. She couldn't get enough of him.

"Easy, you two," Cole called from across the aisle. "Save it for when we get back. I miss my wife enough as it is."

Becca laughed and snuggled into Dom's shoulder instead. Even Dom had a job waiting for him back home.

"You don't think I'm letting you get away that easily, do you?" Pat had said one night at the hotel in Panama. "I'm always on the lookout for good operatives."

At first, Dom had been hesitant.

"It's been a long haul this time," he admitted. "I could use a break."

"I'll give you a month," Pat had promised. "But then you're mine. The unit needs you."

Blade, who managed the operational side of the business, had reassured him that most of the projects they took on were for the U.S. government, even if they were deniable.

"We go where regular forces can't—either for political reasons or because it's not a sanctioned op—and we pick and choose our missions. The money's good, and we've all got each other's backs. Several of us have worked together before, in the SEALs or the Army."

Dom hadn't needed long to think about it. "That's reason enough for me."

"Welcome to the team," Cole had said as they toasted Dom that night—or Ghost, as Pat and the others called him.

Hearing them call him Ghost was a strange reminder for Becca. She'd always known him as Dom—the man she'd fallen for, the one who had saved her, cared for her. Ghost felt like someone else. A shadow of the past she hadn't really known, a part of him she was only just beginning to understand. That name belonged to the soldier, the man who had spent years operating in the world's most dangerous corners, surviving impossible odds. She'd seen glimpses of that side of him when he stormed the hacienda to rescue her. It wasn't just a nickname. It was who he'd been before they met—the man capable of disappearing into the night and coming back with victory on his shoulders.

It made her love him more, realizing he wasn't just Dom, her protector, but Ghost too—the man who could walk through fire to protect the people he loved. And while she might never fully know all the things he'd done or the places he'd been, she didn't need to. Whoever he was out there in the field, to her, he'd always be Dom.

Becca had seen the delighted expression on his face and knew he'd made the right decision. Sure, it was dangerous work, but that's what he was trained for and what he was good at. He was a soldier, and like all soldiers, he needed a challenge. He'd be bored doing anything else. That was just who he was, and she had no desire to change him.

"I feel like I'm going to wake up one day and realize this has all been a dream," she murmured into his neck, breathing in his scent.

He stroked her hair. "Then I'm going to remind you every day that it's not."

She laughed. "Deal."

Turns out she'd been wrong—there was such a thing as a happy ending. She and Dom were living proof.

WHAT'S NEXT?

Want more Blackthorn Security? Take a look at the next book in the addictive romantic suspense series.

STEEL VENGEANCE

GEMMA FORD

STEEL VENGEANCE

A personal vendetta takes a surprising turn in this thrilling, second-chances romantic scorcher by Amazon bestselling author, Gemma Ford.

When former army doctor Stitch's peaceful, new life is shattered by a lethal Taliban attack, the ex-special forces operative is catapulted back into the dangerous world he left behind. With only one thought in his mind: Vengeance.

Rookie agent, Sloane has been with the CIA for two months. This is her first overseas assignment and she's way out of her depth. But she's onto something—and it might be the biggest cover-up the agency has ever seen.

Enter Stitch, the angry former special forces soldier with a personal vendetta who threatens to destroy the mission. They join forces with a common goal, but when things take a lethal turn, can she count on him or will he sacrifice the mission for his own personal blood lust?

This is a steamy, second-chances, military romance with themes of revenge, betrayal and past trauma - and a guaranteed happily ever after!

Available on Amazon and Kindle Unlimited.

CHAPTER 1

PESHAWAR, PAKISTAN

Stitch trailed Abdul Omari as he and his entourage moved toward the local coffee shop. They moved as a unit, Omari dead center, surrounded by his four muscle-bound bodyguards. They wore the traditional shalwar kameez, hiding who knows what kind of firepower underneath. From the bulges, it was clear they were packing.

Omari had shaved off the beard he'd sported back home in Afghanistan, trying to change up his profile. He'd also cut his curly hair short and ditched the hat. A high-value target on the U.S. radar, he was flying under it now. That's why he'd holed up in this part of Pakistan.

But not low enough.

Peshawar was near the Afghan-Pakistan border and chaotic enough for the warlord to disappear in. The streets were crowded, markets buzzing, traffic non-stop. Recent bombings and political unrest made it a prime spot for someone looking to vanish.

Stitch stepped back as a rickshaw rattled by.

He scanned his six, making sure no one had clocked him. Everything seemed normal—locals doing their thing, vendors barking deals, taxis and rickshaws dodging potholes, and women with shopping bags, their heads wrapped in hijabs or scarves.

Then, his eyes locked onto a woman in a dusky blue headscarf over a shalwar kameez. She carried a canvas bag, her dark hair resting over one shoulder. Unlike the other women, who were either chatting or keeping their heads down, this one moved solo, eyes dead ahead—right at the target.

Omari.

No mistake. Her eyes were uncovered, sharp, and locked in. She moved fluidly, stopping now and then to look at the produce, casually picking up an item here or there, dropping it in her bag. But her attention kept snapping back to Omari, tracking him.

At first, Stitch chalked it up to coincidence. Maybe she was just headed in the same direction—these streets were always packed. But three days straight? No way. She was tailing Omari, same as him.

Omari disappeared into the café. The dirty glass windows, covered with Arabic script, blocked the view. Stitch crossed the street, zeroing in on a teahouse that gave him a good vantage point.

Like the locals, Stitch was dressed to blend. His beard and deep tan made him fit right in. Back in the Afghan mountains, people thought he was one of them. The only thing that could give him away was his eyes—icy, intense blue. But today, with the sun blazing, his shades took care of that.

He ordered tea, paid the guy, and settled outside. Two men beside him were playing a game that looked like backgammon. Stitch watched them roll the dice, move their pieces across the beat-up board.

The woman had the same idea. She strolled into the shop next door, scanning an array of colorful scarves. She took her sweet time, trying a few on, admiring herself in the mirror by the entrance. Stitch could see her reflection. Behind her, the shopkeeper hovered, ready to make the sale.

After some haggling, she grabbed a cream-colored scarf, bought it, and swapped it for the blue one.

Smart, Stitch thought. Swapping her look like that. Anyone watching her would probably mistake her for someone else.

But not him.

Now, Stitch kept tabs on both her and Omari, who was tucked away inside the café. She moved on to the next shop, passing in front of him, not even sparing him a second glance. With his head bowed over his cup of tea, sunglasses on, she probably wrote him off as just another local.

Behind the shades, he studied her closer. Her skin was lighter than he'd thought. She wasn't from here, even if she'd nailed the look. Her clothes were perfect, obviously bought locally, and she wore the scarf like a pro. Her hair, a rich chocolate brown, fell straight down her back. He'd seen a flash of it when she'd swapped scarves.

Her lips had that natural pout, like something straight out of an old cartoon. Betty Boop, minus the lipstick. They sat perfectly on her heart-shaped face, framed by big, kohl-lined eyes.

Stitch wasn't about to jump to conclusions. She could be one of Omari's mistresses—word was, the drug lord had more than a few. Maybe she thought Omari was messing around with another woman. Not a stretch, knowing his type. Then again, maybe she was playing a different game.

Maybe she wasn't local at all. Could be CIA. Could be MI6. Omari was a hot ticket for any intel agency.

He eavesdropped as she spoke to the shopkeeper, asking about something.

Pashto. She had it down pretty well, but a few words were off.

Stitch frowned.

Who the hell was she?

A black SUV rolled up outside the café. Three men stepped out—two with beards and skull caps, the third clean-shaven with a military haircut. The woman pulled out her phone, pretending to snap a selfie while holding up a necklace to her chest.

Stitch wasn't buying it. Her camera was pointed right at the men.

He took a sip of tea, mind racing.

She lingered for another twenty minutes, hopping between shops until it became obvious she was stalling. When she was done, she finally headed off.

Making a split-second decision, he got up and tailed her.

She moved with intent now, mission complete. No more playing the shopper. Twice, she checked over her shoulder, scanning for a tail. She'd had some training, no question. But she didn't see him. Stitch had spent a lifetime blending into shadows.

Rounding a corner, she made her way to an old, beat-up Honda scooter. Stitch watched as she hopped on, slinging the shopping bag across her chest.

Damn. He was on foot.

He threw himself in front of a rickshaw, forcing the driver to slam the brakes. Stitch jumped in, barking, "Follow that scooter!"

The driver shot him a weird look but hit the gas, swerving around a delivery van coming straight at them.

She didn't go far. Four streets later, she slowed, hopped the sidewalk, and parked in front of a butcher shop. Dead carcasses hung from hooks inside.

A mile, if that. Barely worth the chase.

Stitch paid the driver and got out. She slipped into a plain door next to the shop.

He glanced up at the building. Was this where she lived? Or some kind of safe house?

Stitch took in the crumbling structure with its sagging balconies that looked ready to collapse. If it was a front, it was a damn good one. The smell of raw meat mixed with the thick exhaust fumes, while flies buzzed overhead.

This part of town was more industrial—leatherworkers, jewelers, and other trades. But it was still packed. Wires crisscrossed the narrow streets, draped with laundry and flags.

No way to tell which apartment she went into. He could've followed her in, but without knowing where she was headed, it'd be a waste.

The building was climbable. Plenty of footholds. But broad daylight wasn't the time for it.

So, he circled the block, taking in every angle.

Failing to plan is planning to fail, his old special forces instructor used to say. Prep was key. That mentality had stuck with Stitch long after he left the service. His wife used to tease him about it.

You need to be more spontaneous, she'd joke. But she had enough spontaneity for both of them.

Soraya.

He closed his eyes, letting the grief hit him, sharp and familiar. Then, he took a breath, shoving it back down.

Soon. Omari was going to pay for what happened to her.

But first, Stitch had to figure out who this woman was

and what she wanted with Omari. He didn't need any more complications.

After making his rounds, he found a bench up the street and sat down to wait.

* * *

Enjoyed the extract? *Steel Vengeance* is now available from Amazon and Kindle Unlimited here: www.amazon.com/dp/B0DFB2XY9J.

ABOUT THE AUTHOR

Gemma Ford is a romantic suspense novelist who enjoys writing about feisty, independent women and their brave, warm-hearted men. *Duty Bound* is the first book in Gemma's Blackthorn Security romantic suspense series.

You can browse the rest of the series or sign up to Gemma's mailing list for discounts, promos and the occasional freebie at her website: www.authorgemmaford.com.

www.ingramcontent.com/pod-product-compliance
Lightning Source LLC
LaVergne TN
LVHW021701060526
838200LV00050B/2448